A HOPE FULFILLED

A NOVELLA OF BIBLICAL EDOM AND OBADIAH'S PROPHECY

APRIL W GARDNER

Enjoy the story! *April G.*

Big Spring Press

4 - 24

Scripture quotations taken from the King James Version unless otherwise indicated.

Cover design: Indie Cover Design

ISBN-13:978-1-945831-40-9

Library of Congress Control Number: 2023913229

A Hope Fulfilled: a novella of Biblical Edom and Obadiah's prophecy

Published by Big Spring Press.

San Antonio, Texas, United States of America.

CONTENTS

Acknowledgements   V

Forward   VI

Series Details   VIII

Cast of Characters   X

Chapter 1   1

Chapter 2   13

Chapter 3   25

Chapter 4   42

Chapter 5   55

Chapter 6   68

Chapter 7   84

Chapter 8   90

Chapter 9   100

Chapter 10   117

Chapter 11   131

What to Read Next   149

About the Author   150

Knowing Obadiah Preview   151

ACKNOWLEDGEMENTS

Dedication

To the women of my small group at Oakwood Baptist. As I wrote, each of you was on my mind. Thank you for your unfailing love and support and for your countless prayers.

Acknowledgments

As ever, God gets first credit. Thank you, Lord, for the inspiration and for providing every word of this series. Mom, literally couldn't have done it without you. Your experience, wisdom, and insightful content helped make this series what it is. I'm proud to put your name next to mine on the cover of *But in Mount Zion*. Others who contributed with invaluable feedback and who deserve oodles of thanks: my faithful writing partners Tanya Eavenson and Rebekah Gyger, my brilliant editor Lesley McDaniel, and advanced readers Dr. S. Rosenburg, Charlotte, Susan, Jennifer W., and Jennifer C. Thank each of you for your time, your input, and your dedication to excellence.

FORWARD

This story was inspired by the Old Testament prophecy of Obadiah. It is _not_ meant to teach or interpret, but to direct the reader toward their own investigation of Scripture. For that, check out _Knowing Obadiah_, my commentary for Christian women.

Another quick note for those unfamiliar with the prophecy. _Nothing_ is known about the author, Obadiah, apart from the fact he wrote the little book. _When_ he wrote it is also in question, but most Bible scholars agree that the events related in the prophecy point to the fall of Jerusalem to the Babylonians in 587 BC (Obad. 10–14), which would mean the prophesied destruction of Edom (Obad. 4–9) would have taken place thirty-some years later when Babylon then destroyed Edom.

Because the book of Obadiah gives so little about the author and events surrounding his prophecy, my imagination had lots of room to roam. Please, take this novella in the sense it is intended—as one author's idea of what _might_ have happened. I pray that it will whet your appetite for more of this book of the Bible, and that you'll soon find yourself digging into personal study.

~ April W Gardner

SERIES DETAILS

A Fire and a Flame

- *A Hope Fulfilled*, a novella of biblical Edom and Obadiah's prophecy

- *Knowing Obadiah*, a Christian Women's Bible Commentary

- *But in Mount Zion*, a companion study for *Knowing Obadiah* (personal or small group)

Can be read in any order. Learn more and purchase at www.aprilgardner.com/fireandflame.

Visit author's website and subscribe for these gifts:
www.aprilgardner.com/fireandflame-freebies

1. Beautiful in His Sight, a Christian WWI Romance set during the Halifax Explosion. (e-book). *Jack is her freedom. Silas, her salvation. God? He's the building that buries her.*

2. The Red Feather, Christian Native American Historical (ebook and digitally narrated audio). *Amidst the clash of weapons, two lives intertwine in a battle for love, faith, and survival.* Experience a vivid frontier setting and an enemies-to-lovers story that will render you breathless.

CAST OF CHARACTERS

(in order of appearance)

Tikvah bat Aharon, enslaved Hebrew woman

Sawaha: enslaved Edomite laundress

Shimshon: enslaved Hebrew

Jalam: miller's son

General Belibni: Babylonian

Captain Namtar: Babylonian

Duke Zerah: Edomite, Tikvah's enslaver

Kala ben Mahlon: Hebrew guard/liaison

Aos: overseer of Zerah's enslaved

Matron Houda: Edomite, Zerah's wife

Chapter 1

*The vision of Obadiah. Thus saith the Lord
God concerning Edom; We have heard a ru-
mour from the Lord, and we sent an ambas-
sador among the heathen, Arise ye, and let us
rise up against her in battle.* (Obad. 1)

"Late are you, Jewess? Do you not remember what
happens to those of your kind who rebel?"

Tikvah ignored the laundress's taunt and, arms trembling from exertion, continued across the courtyard and
out to the master's mule shed. Around the back of it,
she dumped the kitchen's overflowing cinder bucket into
the manure pile. Clouds of ash belched into the dusky
pre-dawn air. Coughing, she swatted at the dust and spun
back toward the house.

In the courtyard, the laundress remained kneeling at
the fire pit, working sparks over straw kindling. A pile of

crumpled robes sat beside her. If the laundress had already begun her day of scrubbing, Tikvah indeed ran late.

And Tikvah *bat* Aharon, daughter of Aharon and of Zion, was never late.

She sped past the laundress, praying to avoid confrontation, but the woman's taunt pursued her.

"What excuse will you give the overseer while he retrieves the lash, eh?"

Tikvah's shoulders cringed upward, but she would not be drawn into an argument. Instead, she tossed a reply over her shoulder as she went. "I stayed up late polishing serving bowls."

Not that the matron would accept such an excuse for tardiness, and this was not a morning to test her thin patience. Even now, she screeched for her chambermaid. Her shrill commands, carried through the windows above and clashed with the laundress's cruel laughter.

Shuddering, Tikvah shut the kitchen door on both rackets and made straight for the stone heating over coals for the morning's flat bread. She wrenched off her sooty headscarf and lowered to her knees beside the bowl of dough. The required stack of round, unleavened flatbread must number three score before she could rise again.

By the time she darted outside again with the two flatbreads she'd set aside, the sun crested the far ridges of the Al Sil range. She entered an empty, narrow alley between dwellings. One direction ended against the city wall and the red-streaked sky above. Nothing lay beyond it but jagged cliffs and empty air. The other way, the alley's exit led down into the city, its smooth packed dirt a cool kiss to the soles of Tikvah's bare feet.

The heights on which the village, Busayra, stood did not celebrate the warmth of summer in the manner of the scorching valley. Tikvah wore a shawl in the mornings, while the residents in the scattered villages of the lowlands fanned themselves from sunup.

But something more insidious encroached upon the horizon than oppressive heat. Frantic whispers trailed up from the valley clear to the master's house in the heights with a message of dread.

The armies of Babylon had arrived.

Not the biannual caravan of the tribute collector. Not a roving, policing cohort sent to verify duty to pledges of obedience. But the king himself escorted by the bulk of his standing army.

Tikvah's stomach clenched, her face undecided about a frown or a smile. The matron's piercing voice—orders for the cook—shot into the alley and decided for her.

Smile it was, for a prophecy foretelling Edom's doom awaited its hour in the light of fulfillment.

Hope was a slippery, dangerous thing.

Brisk morning air freshened Tikvah's overheated cheeks as she clutched the wrapped bread to her chest and took the downward switchback lanes at speed. The distance from the master's residence on the peak to the grain mill by the city gate was not so far, but Tikvah stuck to winding, little-trod paths. And in a village hewed from mountain-top sandstone, one did not go anywhere in too great a hurry. Except a slave woman such as herself whose skin would pay for any delay in return.

Her breath came hard by the time she swung the last corner and let herself into the miller's yard through the back gate. The toasted-grass scent of crushed grain flooded her senses. Wafts of donkey dung mingled in to give the mill its peculiar aroma. The courtyard opened before her, the only segment of the city in which she felt a semblance of welcome.

Although, this morning, there was none to greet Tikvah but the dogs. Hind ends wagging, they yipped and snuffled and bounced, each eager for attention. She stopped and absently scratched at a furry ear.

A glance about informed her that the open-sided mill house stood vacant. Another showed no feet under the privy door. The miller and his wife often slept through the morning hours, but Shimshon would not abandon his post.

"Fair morning to you," she called and listened with care for his wordless acknowledgment.

Nothing. Only the cluck of chickens from two yards over and the impatient murmur of those outside the city wall, waiting for the gate master to arrive, key in hand.

Was Shimshon still abed? Apart from his sleeping shed, he could be in no other place. She began that way.

The shuffle of feet drew her gaze to the exterior stairway leading from the miller's dwelling.

The miller's young son, Jalam, rubbed his eyes as he trudged down the last stair of their upper-story apartment. He yawned and turned for the donkey's stall below their abode. "Where is Shimshon?"

"I was about to ask you the same."

The donkey's bray drowned half of Tikvah's reply. Just as well. Jalam wouldn't have answered.

The sleeping shed, a low stone structure slung against the city wall and topped by bundled branches, housed three dogs and one Hebrew male. That male's tattered brown robe peeked out from the opening.

Tikvah set Shimshon's wrapped bread on the shed's roof and bent to peer into the deep shadows. He lay curled in a ball, hugging himself against the cold of the desert night. Soft snores revealed that her old friend hadn't expired in the night. Relief rushed through her, dampened by her notice of his absent blanket. Yahweh be thanked for the dogs and their faithful warmth, fleas notwithstanding.

Reaching in, she jostled his knee. "*Abba*. Abba! It is morning." Tikvah couldn't remember when she first started calling him *abba*, meaning father, but the term fit as well as it did the man who'd sired and raised her to the young age of eight. Never mind that their traditional roles of caretaker and dependent were reversed.

Shimshon startled and shoved up on an elbow. "Eeh-ah?"

"Yes, it is I, Tikvah. Miller Reuel has yet to come down, but dawn has come and gone."

Grunting agreement, Shimshon scooted out of the shed on his backside. His head emerged, the streaks of gray in his brown hair catching the sun's first rays. He used the structure's stone to aid himself to standing.

Though she grimaced at his struggle, Tikvah stayed back.

A man, even a muted and blinded slave, had his pride. Shimshon couldn't be over forty years of age, but a decade of hard labor and poor sleep had beaten his body down. Hunched, he swatted dust and straw from his garment.

Dog fur lifted into the wind, and Tikvah batted it from her nose.

Shimshon fussed next over his shaggy beard, then his hair, raking fingers through it and retying it at his nape.

Tikvah pulled a missed blade of straw from his whiskers. "Handsome as ever."

He snorted as though it were a jest, but she'd meant it. If she looked past his sunken orbs and weathered skin, she could see the attractive man he'd once been.

"Hungry?" she asked, chipper.

He nodded but gestured toward the privy.

She waited for him to take the well-worn trail, there and back, then collected his food off the top of the shed and walked with him to the low stone wall that served as enclosure for the donkey. Shimshon's head hung, his feet dragged, and there was a distinct limp in his right leg. Had he hurt himself, or were his joints still working out nighttime kinks?

Asking would get her nowhere, and his absent tongue would not be blamed. This she'd learned from years of delivering his meals. Shimshon was not one to complain about aches. Neither did he mope over his lot. So what was this dejection she sensed in him? Either years of enslavement had caught up to him at last, or this signaled something else. Tikvah suspected she knew which.

She took him by the elbow to halt him before he stubbed his toe against the wall. Concern overturned her mouth. The man knew this yard like one did the top of their mouth. She wrung the worry from her voice and guided him to sitting. "It was frightfully cold last night. What has become of your blanket?"

The miller and his wife were not the kindest sorts, but neither were they cruel, and Jalam was too lazy to torment a mutilated slave.

Duty bound, Shimshon took the bread she nudged against his arm, then made a waggling motion at the top of his head, as of a floppy ear, their sign for *dog*.

"Ah. I should have known. Which one was it? Roach? I bet it was Roach. He is the stealing type, rotten beast."

Hearing his name, the black-coated dog loped over, ears flapping, and stuck his nose against Shimshon's bread before she could swat him away.

"See!" She laughed, giving the accused a scratch under his chin. "What did I tell you? He would steal the freckles from your face if he thought they would be tasty."

Shimshon shrugged, staring down into his dish with his sightless sockets. The image of her resilient friend appearing so crestfallen sobered her.

She wrapped an arm around his thin shoulders. "I am sorry you passed such a dreary night, but take heart. With the evening meal, I will bring another blanket." Her own, if she must.

Head lifting, he donned a fleeting smile and patted his chest.

"Thank me by eating." She tapped his untouched bread and tried again to brighten his spirits. "We cannot have you losing strength. Or shivering to your death. Not with the summer harvest at hand. Then the donkey might have to earn his keep for a change." She wasted effort on another light laugh.

Shoulders slumped, he put an obligatory bite into his mouth and began the laborious process of chewing it down.

Beyond the walled mill and house, the city was coming awake. The shriek of the gate's hinges announced that city business was in session. Patrons, farmers up from the valley desiring to sell their grain, could arrive at the mill at any moment.

"The gate will soon be opening." Then the day's rush would begin, and he would pull the millstone around its endless circuit on an empty stomach. "Hurry, my friend."

Ordering him about rarely worked to accomplish her purpose, that of keeping him alive and hale. Neither did calling him Shimshon, the name given him in mockery after his capture. And using his true name had only ever resulted in trouble for them both. She had long ago put it from her mind.

When her urgings produced her precise expectations, she sighed and settled in. "While you are picking at that bread, you can tell me why your spirits are low. I'd have thought our news would put a grin on that face."

Shimshon angled his head toward her. A knot formed on his brow, and he grunted a single "Uh."

"You have not heard?"

"Uh!"

"You have not heard! How have you not heard?"

He shoved at her knee. "Uh, uh!"

The man's eyes and tongue might have been absent, but those ears missed nothing. Or so she'd always thought.

At the chance to share the news, a thrill sang in Tikvah's blood. She flitted a glance at Jalam lounging in the hay pile. Then, in the true manner of a gossip, she leaned near and lowered her voice, lest it carry her nervous excitement where it should not go. "It is King Nabonidus. His armies have arrived at last!"

Shimshon sat upright with such suddenness their heads clocked together. Neither paused to care. His jostle of her arm demanded she continue.

A girlish giggle escaped her, but who could blame a slave for giddy hopes? "There is little more I can tell. As ever, news is slow to reach me, but the house is chaotic with preparations. The matron has been screeching since before dawn. Snapping at anyone not moving at an all-out dash. And the duke, our master? Nowhere about. Gone down the mountain, I say. Mark me, abba. Before long, perhaps as early as tomorrow's high sun, we will receive visitors. Important ones. What do you say to *that*, sir?"

The title left her on a silly note, but they both knew she meant it with all her heart.

In times as these, when she put such weighty questions to him, she was not addressing the slave who dragged the millstone but the man who'd strode nobly through the city gate ten summers before, purpose driving his steps. Before the sun set on that day, he had been in chains.

He'd kept his tongue for a month of days, but when it refused to cease wagging, Aos had removed it on their master's furious order. In those too-few days, Tikvah came to know Shimshon well. She had peered into his eyes and seen his heart. It beat with unerring devotion to Yahweh, and over the succeeding years, in the times when her child-like faith flagged, it had been the only strength to hold her upright.

Now, a slow, cautious smile climbed his lips. It could mean anything.

She waited, breath shallow, and admonished herself not to press him. His reply would not be rushed. Face lifted to the warming sun and the heavens beyond, he held there. If he had eyes, they would surely be closed in prayer.

At long last, he turned his head back toward her, the smile still in place, though grown. He held out his hand and when she slipped hers inside, he squeezed it and gave a tiny shake. "Eeh-ah." His sound for her name.

"Yes?"

"Eeh-ah!"

She stared at their joined hands, trying to work out what he tried in his rudimentary way to tell her. "Forgive me. I do not follow your meaning."

Releasing her, he slid off the wall and squatted. With a crooked finger, he wrote a single word in the sand. Tikvah.

Her name. But also...

"Tikvah." The word, her own name, left her on an exhale. For its meaning, hope, was almost too dear, too fragile to voice.

And yet, her stomach leaped with it.

Tikvah. Hope.

Dared she believe it, embrace it? After all, one could aim hope any sort of direction. This hope scribbled in the dirt might not be The Hope they had been praying for.

Shimshon didn't leave her wondering. He scooted right, and with big, bold strokes, formed another word beside the first: kala.

Tikvah. Kala.

Hope. Fulfill.

Chapter 2

All the men of thy confederacy have brought thee even to the border: the men that were at peace with thee have deceived thee, and prevailed against thee; they that eat thy bread have laid a wound under thee: there is none understanding in him. (Obad. 7)

Babylonian generals were every bit as barbarically splendid, as beautifully hideous as Tikvah had always imagined. At least, this one was.

General Belibni.

And yet, he disregarded the typical attire of his class: heavy adornment, elaborate headdress, long-fringed robe. General Belibni indulged in none of these.

Wine vessel between her sweating palms, Tikvah stood next to the niche where the household gods resided. From that position, she kept one eye on the ground at her feet and one on the general's relaxed form, ever ready at his slightest twitch to serve. He reclined in the place of honor at Duke Zerah's spread.

Her master, Duke Zerah, partook of the evening meal on his rooftop under the stars. With him sat his three lord-generals, his two grown sons, and two distinguished—albeit privately hated—guests: General Belibni, the king's sharpest weapon, and Captain Namtar, the general's right hand. The only two who truly mattered were the Babylonian general and his captain, but Tikvah, as wine bearer, monitored eight in all.

Nine if one included the not-so-distinguished foot soldier who accompanied the Babylonians. The man leaned a shoulder in repose against a wooden column of the jasmine-strung pergola that covered the small gathering. Torchlight flickered in the cuffs adorning his forearms.

Tikvah loosed a soft huff. Even the lowly soldier wore more jewelry than the general. And some guard he was, yawning at his post. The occasional glance toward the door leading down was the sum of his soldierly attention.

Was the Babylonian general so confident of his safety among the Edomites? If he'd gleaned even a word of Master Zerah's perpetual curses on his overlords, General Belibni might have rethought leaving his sword outside the house.

Of course, to recline at her master's offered spread while armed would have been the height of offense. The sharing of a meal was a covenant of peace and brotherhood. But should a Babylonian general care?

Tikvah thought not. Especially not one who accompanied a mighty king on a campaign of violence.

King Nabonidus's aim, so said the updated report, was to reach the desert oasis of Tayma in Arabia. The kingdom of Edom lay in his path. The question passed from whispering lip to trembling ear was whether the halt of his army in their lowlands was to resupply their stores...or whether the king's tolerance for Master Zerah's skimmed tributes had reached its limit.

Privy to prophecy, Tikvah recognized the true purpose of King Nabonidus's presence in the valley; although, such knowledge did nothing to ease the fatigue cramping her lower back.

The night grew interminable. Perspiration dampened her hairline and accumulated under the palms holding the wine vessel snug against her abdomen. It weighed considerably less than at the outset, its effects discernible in the Babylonian captain's bellows of laughter.

Face tipped high, Captain Namtar's long black hair swished over his back as he laughed.

While the captain displayed boundless energy, his general appeared like a sprawling tiger, silent and watching. General Belibni reclined on a straw mat, a single cushion supporting his upper body. She had offered him several others, but he'd refused. Did he wish to prove his hardiness? Or to remove hindrances should swift defensive action be required?

Little chance of the latter. His army, twelve thousand strong, might be camped below in the valley, but this tiger, black eyes on perpetual scan, gave the impression it would take a multitude to bring him down.

In the manner of a trusted guest, he'd surrendered his weapons for the evening, but an ocean of bloodshed still swam in those blade-sharp eyes. And where his captain sported the bangles, brass girdle, and vibrantly colored draping linens of their elite class, General Belibni's only adornments were his scars and scabbing wounds.

The sole exception was a broad girdle, crafted of simple leather, wrapping his waist. It boasted no etching, unless one counted its myriad slash marks, the work of an enemy sword, no doubt. Or many of them.

A shiver of fear raced down Tikvah's spine, but she squelched it. This was the man Yahweh had chosen. Though she had no assurance of surviving whatever lay ahead, she would stand firm and trust the God of her fathers. The God who'd given her and Shimshon the strength to rise every morning and worship despite their pain and humiliation.

Eyes fluttering closed, she uttered a swift prayer. *If You require an instrument to accomplish Your purpose, I am Your servant, my living God and everlasting King.*

"Would you believe it?" Captain Namtar's booming voice flashed Tikvah's eyes open again.

He spoke in the Akkadian that Master Zerah had compelled her to learn, along with the rest of his serving slaves, any who might have direct contact with their overlords. So they might better serve their esteemed visitors.

By *visitors*, he meant the delegates and accompanying legions who toured the region to collect tribute and ensure all subjects lived in compliance with Babylonian rule. And by *esteemed*, of course, he meant feared, loathed, and wished rotting in their tombs.

Captain Namtar continued speaking through a laugh that he struggled to contain. "There I found myself on a pebble of an island in the middle of Egypt's great river, surrounded by roaring crocodiles in full heat of the mating season, and not a weapon to my person but that mal-crafted slingshot."

Thunderous laughter filled the chamber, Master Zerah's the loudest. His lord-generals and sons rivaled him for obnoxious pandering to the captain's humor. Only General Belibni, who sipped his wine, did not engage, though his keen gaze roved the chamber.

Still cackling, Master Zerah elbowed Captain Namtar beside him. "Did you use it to peg one of the overgrown lizards in the eye? Come, tell us of your heroic escape."

"Nay! Indeed, not. There was more use in scratching my backside with that cracked slingshot than in hitting anything." The captain upended his goblet into his mouth, then gulped and held it high, red dribbling into his groomed beard.

Tikvah shot off the wall, feet swift and silent, and rushed up the channel created between his outstretched body and that of her master. The captain's heat penetrated the thin fabric of her gown, his oiled black hair putting off the scent of almonds.

She bent, and liquid shivered from the vessel's spout and into his cup.

He seemed not to notice her nerves, for he'd gone on regaling them with his story. "The river beasts have stumps for legs, you see, and cannot climb. So I scaled the isle's only sizable stone and stood on tiptoe. Much like a girl climbing the nearest object to flee a roach." Mouth open wide, he guffawed at his own cowardice.

Tikvah's eyes shot to the general for his censure but found him at last wearing a lazy smile, as if amused by his captain's ridiculous behavior, then and now. A brush to her skin jerked her attention back down. The captain, who'd noted her lingering, granted himself a liberal touch. The lightest trace of a finger across the curve of her ankle.

Her heart stammered, indignation and fear sending it into a fit. Then her feet were shuffling backward, moving before her brain could caution her otherwise. She rushed back to her post, her kneecaps trembling.

A displeased frown eclipsed the captain's mouth, but praise Yahweh, Master Zerah diverted his attention by bursting into a dozen robust denials of the tale's cowardly turn. He would not believe such a thing of General Belibni's most honored soldier, the master declared. He would not so much as imagine it. No, he would not.

"In truth, I did," Captain Namtar asserted, goblet back at his lips.

"I quaked with fear through the night," he went on, "and hailed the first passing barque revealed by the day's light. And I defy any here to act otherwise when stranded on the breeding grounds of twoscore bull crocodiles. There! You have it in full. Now, you may judge my heroism."

"Of a certainty, Captain Namtar. None here judge harshly." Master Zerah offered him the platter of sesame cakes. "Without doubt, twoscore river beasts are the limit of courage for any man."

"Ah, the gracious host." Captain Namtar thrust his drinking arm high again, as if in toast. "Girl!"

Already? The general could not approve of his captain debasing himself in such a fashion. Against her bidding, Tikvah's gaze skipped to Namtar's superior.

General Belibni, eyes already on her, quirked a thick black eyebrow as if to say, *what have I to do with it?*

Tikvah's heart leaped into her throat, her feet into motion. In the next blink, she was at the captain's side, and he was lowering his drinking vessel, switching it to the opposite hand. The action freed the one on her side to wrap around her ankle in a shackling hold.

Her breath caught. Red liquid sloshed in the base of her pitcher.

Hot and calloused, those errant fingers slid up her calf. "In what *other* ways are you generous, Duke Zerah?" Somehow, the captain's voice had lost its drunken slur. This man knew precisely what he did.

Lord God of Heaven! Is this Your plan?

You are mine, Daughter.

Indeed, she was Yahweh's alone. So why did she stand there letting another claim her?

Spine stiffening, Tikvah twisted in place. The movement wrenched her from the captain's possession. She gave the room her back as she marched to her post, spun in place, and looked straight ahead at the wall opposite.

I am Yours. Only Yours. Keep me gently, gently. She leaned hard into diligent prayer.

It grew to such a volume in her mind, it took her some moments to realize the room had gone silent, the guard had straightened from his slump, and the master, seething at her, had gone red in the face. Tikvah's throat was a desert, her heart a wounded bird floundering behind her ribs.

The slave overseer, Aos, emerged from the shadows, eyes bright with glee behind thick lids. Though a slave himself,

a coil of leather sat upon his hip, as ever it did, sashed
there by the scarlet rope wrapped about his waist. "Do you
require my services, Master?" he asked, the nasal whine of
his voice never more irritating.

Flicking Aos a meaningful glance, Master Zerah rose
to his feet, then bowed low at the waist in the captain's
direction. "Forgive my household this offense, most esteemed Captain Namtar. The Jews have always believed
themselves above us. This slave is no exception."

The lounging guard took one step away from his post
but halted at the lift of the general's hand.

"Yes, yes, take the Jewess," her master urged. "Have her
in your chamber to do with as Your Excellency's good
pleasure dictates."

His eldest son looked on over the brim of his cup as if
he might hide his developing grin, for Master Zerah's true
intent was obvious to all on the roof but his guests.

The curse related to her was no secret. Even his generals
watched animatedly, gazes shifting between the belliger-
ents, their eagerness for violence almost palpable. One or
two had been present when Shimshon issued his warning
all those years ago. Before Shimshon lost his tongue to
Master Zerah's wrath, he'd raised his arms high and stated
in tone of decree that if any man touched Tikvah's purity
without her consent, their God—the same who'd flooded
a wicked world and turned the disobedient to salt—would
exact justice upon him.

None would ever accuse Master Zerah of intelligence, but in this, he'd found brains enough to heed. Until now. Of course, *he* would not be the one tainting her and cursing himself, but his enemy.

While they awaited the general's verdict, every male eye bore into her. Their mixture of shock and greed for cruelty burned through her skin.

But even as heat poured off her body, sweat collecting in every crevice, an unnatural peace settled over her. At her next exhale, her limbs steadied, those cantankerous kneecaps giving up their dance. Then her heart settled into a straight rhythm, and her gaze did not waver from that wall. Whatever the night held, no man would find this daughter of Zion quaking or cowering.

Wordless, his face a mask of nothingness, General Belibni raised his vessel at her.

Tikvah blinked at it.

"What are you waiting for? Serve your lord! Useless girl."

Master Zerah's boom of command rocked her shoulders. Somehow, her body moved, and she found herself tipping her vessel over the general's cup.

"But how steadily she pours." The general's rumbled observation was little more than a murmur, but it may as well have been a lion's roar.

Wise prey, she bowed her head and backed away the instant the last red drop fell.

She'd not gone half a shuffled step when the captain's arm lashed out. He reached up, snatched her by the elbow, and hauled her down beside him. Her knees cracked against the floor, a lock of hair swinging free to dangle in her eyes.

The captain nudged her chin up, then wrapped the lock around a forefinger. "She is no great treat for the eyes, but she does put up a spirited fight. Will you promise to fight me, wench?" His lids drooped, and his breath stank of sour wine.

Nose wrinkling, she angled away.

"It would appear, Namtar," the general said, amused, "she is not afraid of you."

Captain Namtar loosed a mirthless guffaw. "Not afraid of the conqueror of crocodiles?"

Master Zerah swore. "I'll strip the skin from her back. The whip, Aos, bring me the whip!" he shouted, heedless now of the curse.

The captain looked to her master, where he stood frothing with indignation. His left eyebrow arched so comically at her master's display that a puff of air exploded from Tikvah's nose.

A low chuckle rose from the place of honor. "I believe she is not afraid of you either, Zerah."

Tikvah's eyes darted to the general's, confronted the danger stalking their depths, and held. "Why fear the braying ass while the lion charges?" So saying, she let her sight descend to the symbol of Babylon embossed on General Belibni's leather breastplate, the profile of a roaring lion.

Master Zerah spluttered stupidly, but a wicked smile molded the general's hard mouth. "I think...she named asses of you both."

The lazy guard snorted.

Tikvah flashed him a scowl.

For reply, he showed her straight white teeth inside a broad grin.

Captain Namtar released her, a confused frown eclipsing his slack features. He harrumphed, slurring again. "Something should probably be done about that."

"Indeed so!" Hands clasped before him in supplication, Master Zerah bowed repeatedly to each Babylonian in turn. "A thousand apologies, Captain, Your Excellency. The slave has been begging discipline for quite some while. I will have her tongue served up at once." Clawed fingers outstretched, Master Zerah stormed toward her. "Insult my guests, will you, filthy Jewess? I shall teach you to—"

"Halt there." Another raise of the hand, another crash of stillness. General Belibni waved her master off. "My thanks, Zerah. But I prefer my *wenches* intact." Gaze steady on her, he flicked a finger at his guard. "To my chamber with her."

Chapter 3

*How are the things of Esau searched out! How
are his hidden things sought up!* (Obad. 5–6)

Interminable time passed as Tikvah waffled between
sitting sedately on a corner cushion of the master's
unlit guest chamber and pacing before the locked door.
In both, two things did not change: the sweat dampening her brow and her trust in Yahweh.

She paced, eyes closed in prayer, hands in a damp
twist. Any moment, General Belibni would arrive to
begin a true test of her faith. As she awaited whatever
he planned, her thoughts returned again and again to
Shimshon's broad smile, to the words he'd traced into
the dirt.

Tikvah. Kala.

Hope. Expectation.

Fulfill. Finish.

This was God's path, the one He'd chosen for her. For Busayra. For all of Edom. Those facts, blessed as they were, did not lessen the terror of being confronted by King Nabonidus's most feared general.

"Elohim is my refuge and strength." The recitation passed as a whisper over tremulous lips. "A very present help in trouble. Therefore, I will not fear, I will not cower, I will not shake or grovel or—"

The slap of sandals, multiple sets, led to the door. Tikvah swiveled toward the sound.

The door swung wide. Captain Namtar filled the entry, his vibrant, gold-decked attire illuminated by the oil lamp nestled in his large palm. He swept the light in an arc, taking in the chamber—Tikvah with it—in a survey too sharp to be sodden with drink. Where had his stupor gone? She hadn't been locked up *that* long. Had it been an act? That man had consumed enough wine to make it believable.

Satisfied with the state of the room, he pushed through the door and stepped aside.

Behind him, General Belibni emerged from the shadows, his hair and eyes as black as a starless night, his study of her equally dark. A coil of leather hung from the hand that dangled at his thigh. The overseer's preferred whip. Preferred torment.

Tikvah's heart shot straight up her throat. Her feet shuffled backward a step before she caught them and closed her eyes for a one-breath prayer. She was a beloved child of Elohim, Lord Most High. She would *not* cringe before this pagan. No matter the violence that marked his body, lived in his eyes, and shouted from the lithe instrument of torture he held.

"Come forward." His voice, roughened by fatigue or irritation, was the grind of rock on rock. "Out of the shadows, woman, where I might better see that defiance on your face."

Her chin angled up. "Why should I go calmly to that bloody lash?"

His head tipped toward one broad shoulder, a mirthless smile tinkering with the corners of his lips. "Why indeed? Namtar."

The captain set the lamp in a wall niche and arrived at her side in two long strides. He clutched her by the upper arm with hard fingers and jerked her forward into the circle of light sprawled across the floor in front of the general.

Instinct stiffened her legs, her spine. Fury alone wrenched her body against the captain's implacable hold.

"Be *still*." With a forceful move, Captain Namtar arranged her to face that murky smile stretching the general's mouth. At her back now, Namtar held her by both arms, his huffed breath hot and tacky down the back of her neck.

As General Belibni's thick black lashes lowered, his sight trailing her length, she emitted a short growl and gave her shoulders another good thrash. Her loose, rough-woven slave garb hid her form, but the general did not seem to look for curves. When his eyes lifted, they contained the shrewd yet dry assessment of a general inspecting his troops. He directed that gaze over her shoulder to Namtar. "What think you?"

"She is thin."

"Not overly." Gripping her by the waist, the general pinched half a fistful of flesh. "She has meat on her. A bit of cushion besides."

Another thrash dislodged him. "Am I a hog to market, then?"

That irritating half-smile of his reappeared. "No lamb, certainly."

"Her tongue is sharp," the captain contributed, his own tongue once again revealing its wine-taxed slur.

"As is her courage. I recall you saying you approved of her fight."

The captain grunted. "Will she suit, or shall I remove the hook and toss her back in?"

On a purse of the lips, General Belibni stepped back, hand on his chin, as if to consider her from a better angle. For what, she may never guess. Her jaw was loosening to ask when a rapid series of knocks sounded at the door.

At a nod from the general, Captain Namtar admitted their young guard.

The fellow entered, his gaze finding her own in an instant and sticking. A hank of brown hair fell from under his helmet and covered an eye. He left it, seeming more intent on conveying a message than on personal comfort. Or on greeting his superiors.

Leather helmet, shoulder-length hair wavy about his face, short beard covering his cheeks—there wasn't much of his face to be seen, but what was there gripped her with the urgency of a rabbit under the hawk's shadow. Lips parted, he breathed at an unnatural speed, but his legs took the three strides into the room at a light-footed pace.

Might Tikvah say light*hearted* as well? Yes, she might. Because something hovered about his features. An excitement. A brightness, too, that one visible eye widened by something akin to...to...

What was it? Something strange.

Something that did not belong on the expression of a Babylonian, at least not toward chattel, a Hebrew at that.

Something so intense it backed her up, right onto the captain's toes.

On a curse, he released her with a small push toward the guard, the same who had yet to see anything else in the room apart from her.

Wonder. It came to her. That was the thing written across his face. Wonder and, through that tiniest of nods sent her way, reassurance.

Her shoulders lowered a fraction, breath rushing from her lungs. The guard had yet to speak a word, yet soft and soothing, inexplicable peace washed over her spirit, as if Yahweh Himself had entered with the guard.

He smiled then, and Tikvah's lashes fluttered in her confusion.

In like manner, General Belibni glanced between her and the guard. "That is a promising display."

"The best we've seen on this miserable, dust-choked rock." Lip curling, Captain Namtar beat his robes as though to rid himself of said dust.

The general stepped back to set the whip on a side table, the truest *promising display,* to Tikvah's thinking. "What have you there? Uncover anything of use?" He nodded at the objects the guard carried.

Her objects. The few she called her own. Pulse kicking up, she lobbed him an accusing glare. "You went through my things?"

"I...yes." At last, the man broke from his study of her, sight tumbling low where it belonged. Only, it rose again right off, this time landing on the general with a rigidity that bordered on insolence. "Where would you have me put them?"

If the general noticed his inferior's gruff tone, he chose to tolerate it. "Here, give them to me," he said with an impatient wave.

The guard spent the next little while handing her possessions over one at a time. Each received a cursory inspection. A scrap of polished copper she used as a reflecting surface. A twisted-grass necklace crafted by Shimshon. A chipped clay oil lamp, sans oil, with a menorah scratched onto the nozzle. If the master learned of them, he would confiscate them all. And that would be only the beginning of her woes.

Whatever peace she'd found moments before bled from her pores in a torrent of perspiration. "What could you want with those? They are worthless, nothing to you." And yet everything to her. Thankfully, the guard had not found the entirety of her stash.

A soft, agreeing grunt shook General Belibni's chest. "As you say. Worthless." He lifted the lamp to eye level and twisted his wrist so the flickering light brightened the forbidden menorah. "And yet, somehow, I suspect your *braying ass* of a master would show displeasure at this petty rebellion."

Air jetted from her nostrils, careful nonchalance. "What is one more symbol of contempt when he has already vowed to take my tongue?"

"Is there any wonder why?" Captain Namtar said from where he'd propped himself against a wall. Eyes closed and brow rumpled, he looked as if he might regret that last glass of wine he'd demanded of her.

"This is the lot?" The general peered inside the empty lamp and frowned.

The guard hesitated, taking the time to pass her another steady look. Another dose of reassurance.

Which, naturally, had the opposite effect. Why would he feel the need for preemptive calm? Her kneecaps took up wobbling again. He surely had not found... No, it must still be secure. In a score of seasons, none had come close to uncovering it.

The guard's delay snapped General Belibni's head around. "Going soft, Kala?"

"No, my lord," he replied at once. A slight accent garnished his voice, a minor awkwardness about certain sound blends, much like— "There is also this."

Tikvah's heart stopped dead.

The guard jammed two pinching fingers behind his broad leather belt and withdrew the very thing he could not have discovered. Should not have.

With a flick of the wrist, the general tossed the menorah-etched lamp onto the sleeping pallet, then accepted the scrap of rolled parchment extended to him.

"That, that, it is—" *Nothing.* Tikvah's mouth felt numb, her lips stiff about the falsehood she desperately wished to speak. A lie would do her Lord no honor.

But the truth... The truth might kill her.

Peace, Daughter.

As if hearing the Voice, the guard settled into a resting position, arms clasped loose at his back, feet shoulder width apart.

In contrast, Captain Namtar pushed off the wall, renewed interest brightening his dull eyes. "Why do you stutter, little Jewess?"

Tikvah's jaw opened and closed. Her mind lagged two steps behind the men, behind the unraveling details and their various implications. This could be very, very bad. Or it could be the key to her shackles. Her erratic pulse was undecided on which.

With the tips of big fingers, General Belibni unfurled the tiny scroll and scowled at the Hebrew script. Not a moment passed before he shot her a demand. "What is written here?"

She stared at him, eyes growing large and throat shriveling to ash.

Now, Daughter. Speak.

An audible swallow jerked her throat. Moisture coated it, and strength brought unplanned words from her depths. "It is the future, my lord."

General Belibni's black eyebrows stabbed high, the most emotion he'd yet displayed. Had it been her odd statement that surprised him or her suddenly respectful bearing?

A low chuckle filled the chamber. The guard. He looked at her as he'd done since stepping foot into the room.

She fended off the urge to glare back.

"Kala finds your reply amusing," the general said. "Why might that be?"

Kala? The guard's name was Kala? Yes, he'd said that before. But it had flown straight through her ears, in and out again without registering. Now it slammed into her like a punch to the chest.

Hebrew. That name was Hebrew.

She saw it then. The uncurled beard. The odd taint of his Akkadian. Above all, the peculiar interest in her, now explicable.

She saw other things, too. Such as that roaring lion etched into his very Babylonian chest plate. The same lion that devoured their people not twoscore years ago. Starved, devoured, spat out, and left to decay in the fields.

While most of God's Chosen suffered in bondage of one form or another, this one donned the armor of their greatest tormentor, served them, lifted the sword with them. Had he killed Jews with them, too?

Fury barreled through her in a wave of heat. "Because he is rude and ignorant," she bit out. "And a traitor to his people."

Kala flinched, his amiable smile vanishing in a blink. His eyes, though, softened with something she did not like. Despite the fire that her own spat at him, his gaze held her gently. "Not amused, General. Delighted. Grateful. Awed."

"And *not* ignorant." General Belibni gave Tikvah a pointed look, then flapped a dismissive hand. "As for *traitor*, that is for the two of you to work out later."

He returned the curling parchment to Kala. "Enlighten me."

Tikvah's brain stuttered. First, over the notion of *later*. Then, over the command he'd given Kala.

But of course, the man read Hebrew. Of course, he understood the message. Of course, he'd already taken in every word.

And he was delighted. Grateful. Awed.

Her lungs emptied, driven out by a fragment of hope she felt foolish to indulge. She was no closer to understanding what these men wanted, why a Hebrew would be in the Babylonian army, or how she played into any of it. But her odds of getting away from this night with her tongue intact appeared more promising by the moment. There was also the not-at-all-minor detail that none of these men seemed the least interested in the fact that she was a "wench" given over to their whims.

Oh, Lord, the hope of Israel, my refuge, my fortress. Elohai, in you will I trust.

Deep in her prayer, Tikvah startled at the smooth rumble of Kala's voice as he began.

"Hear the word of the Lord, general of Babylon." Ignoring a breathy snort from Captain Namtar, Kala lowered his gaze to the parchment. "And I read. The vision of Obadyah. Thus—"

"A prophecy?" General Belibni broke in.

Kala dipped his chin. "It would appear so, my lord. Visions are a foretelling."

"The wench's supposed *future*," Captain Namtar said.

She imitated Kala's dip of the chin, though absent the respect. "As I said."

"Enough! Read."

Kala met General Belibni's bark of command with instant obedience. "Thus saith Adonoi Hashem concerning Edom. We have heard a report from Hashem, and an envoy is sent among the gentiles, 'Arise ye, and let us rise up against her in battle.'"

General Belibni's raised palm paused the reading. "What does this mean? We *who*? And when was this written?"

Every eye shifted to Tikvah. "The *we* included the prophet, Obadyah, and others like him. Men to whom Adonoi had spoken the message. As for when, Obadyah wrote these words some twelve harvests past."

The general exchanged a meaningful glance with Captain Namtar, whose smirk had melted off. "So long ago..." Upon receiving only a bemused shrug from his captain, the general returned his attention to Tikvah. "And Adonoi is your god?"

"He is the only God."

"Bless His holy name," Kala murmured, to which Tikvah replied on instinct.

"Omein."

They shared a startled glance.

"Touching," the captain said, as dry as Edomite sandstone.

Tikvah wrenched her gaze away. She would not be so hasty to trust this Hebrew, no matter the reverence with which he read.

General Belibni snapped his fingers at Kala. "Read to the end."

"Certainly, my lord." Kala tipped the long sliver of parchment toward the light and cleared his throat. "I have made thee small among the gentles; thou art greatly despised. The pride of thine heart hath deceived thee, thou that dwellest in the clefts of the rock, whose habitation is high; Edom saith in her heart, Who shall bring me down to the ground?"

Captain Namtar's dark chuckle filled the space. "Who but we?"

Kala read on, timbre gaining strength. "Though thou exalt thyself to soar as the eagle, and though thou set thy nest among the stars, thence will I bring thee down, saith Hashem." There, he paused, just long enough for a significant flit of the eye at Captain Namtar. "If thieves came to thee, if robbers by night, oh how art thou cut off! Would they not have stolen only till they had enough? If the grape gatherers came to thee, would they not leave some grapes? How is Esav searched out. How are his hidden treasures pillaged! All the—"

"Hold there," Captain Namtar interrupted. "Who is this Esav?"

"Forefather of the Edomites," Kala supplied before Tikvah could open her mouth.

General Belibni cut his captain a look whetted enough to bow the other man's head in apology and relaunch Kala into translating the prophecy.

"All the men of thy alliance have forced thee and brought thee even to the border; the men that were at peace with thee have deceived thee, and prevailed against thee; they that eat thy bread have laid a trap under thee; there is none detecting it."

The reading picked up speed, General Belibni's lips rising with it, sly and greedy. A jackal circling its prey.

Tikvah's own lips had contemplated curving, though for her, the passage symbolized not destruction and conquest but freedom and the fulfillment of a long-held dream—of the hope to one day live in the land of her fathers. She closed her eyes and moved her tongue along with Kala's, silently reciting the beloved words in Hebrew as he translated.

"Shall I not in that day, saith Hashem, even destroy the wise men out of Edom, and understanding out of the Mount of Esav? And thy mighty men, O Teman, shall be dismayed and lose courage, to the end that every one of the Mount of Esav may be cut off by slaughter. For thy violence against thy brother Ya'akov, shame shall cover thee, and thou shalt be cut off for ever."

The general's chest began rocking with breathy mirth, quiet enough to not disturb the reading. Loud enough to send a train of prickles down Tikvah's spine. This man, this instrument of Yahweh's wrath, would delight in making every word true. Tikvah, however, would be content if she could only lay eyes on Mount Zion.

"In the day that thou stood aloof on the other side," Kala continued, emotion gruff in his throat, "in the day that the strangers carried away captive his forces, and foreigners entered into his gates, and cast lots for Yerushalayim. Even thou wast—" His voice broke.

The sound of it, jagged and ugly, along with the tremble of his jaw, tipped Tikvah's head. The sight did not comply with the Phrygian bonnet on his head or the cloth strips woven about his legs or the broad leather girdle and double-belt encircling his waist. Short of the natural beard, Kala was an Assyrian in every part of his aspect.

But she was aware that appearances could be deceptive. Of their own volition, her feet moved, two shuffled strides that put her to his left. She laid a light hand on his gold-cuffed forearm where he held it aloft.

A soft hiss of surprise passed through his lips.

She was, perhaps, as surprised as he.

He imparted to her a warm look, an expression of gratitude. "What is your name?" he asked on a low thrum, uncaring of the powerful Babylonians looming before them.

"Tikvah." Lingering distrust weakened her voice to a scratchy whisper. "Daughter of Aharon, vinedresser of the Galil." She bit her tongue, not having intended to reveal so much. Something about him had coaxed it out of her.

He mouthed her name, then spoke aloud. "Tikvah. Of course." Eyes shining, he picked back up, voice stouter, louder. "But thou shouldest not have gloated over the day of thy brother in the day of his misfortune; neither shouldest thou have rejoiced over the Bnei Judah in the day of their destruction; neither shouldest thou have spoken proudly in their Day of Trouble."

Drawing breath, he gripped the parchment harder. Tendon and muscle rippled beneath Tikvah's touch. She watched that place where their skin met and marveled at the oddity of this night, at her reckless boldness, and at Kala's ready acceptance of it. Did he realize he leaned ever so gently into her touch?

More pertinent a question: would he think to stop before the end of the passage? Before the prophecy shifted into a promise of ultimate triumph for Israel. Tikvah squirmed where she stood and applied the lightest pressure to his arm.

Intensity not diminished, Kala slowed, as if winding down. "Thou shouldest not have entered into the gate of

My people in the day of their calamity; yea, thou shouldest not have looked down on their affliction in the day of their calamity, nor have laid hands on their substance in the day of their calamity." A hitch, a breath, and a seamless skip forward. "As thou hast done, it shall be done unto thee: thy reward shall return upon thine own head." His voice ground to a stop before he released the scroll's lower half, allowing it to curl up. "That is all." His arms slowly lowered.

Breathing again, she let her hand fall away, her palm now cold. The rest of her chilled when she encountered the general's dancing eyes.

He twirled a finger through a spiral groomed into his long beard. "You believe this prophecy from...Obadyah was it?"

Did he mock her? That cavorting in his eyes could be contempt toward the prophet. Could also be the celebratory feast before executing a hated enemy. Though if the latter, she did not sense her neck would be the one to feel the edge of his sword. Emboldened, she laid a firm hand across her breast. "With my whole heart."

"As do I." Without warning, he bared his teeth in a vicious grin.

"So..." She set her chin at a challenging angle. "What shall we do about it?"

Chapter 4

Thus saith the Lord God; Behold, O mount Seir, I am against thee, and I will stretch out mine hand against thee, and I will make thee most desolate. As thou didst rejoice at the inheritance of the house of Israel, because it was desolate, so will I do unto thee: thou shalt be desolate, O mount Seir, and all Idumea, even all of it: and they shall know that I am the Lord. (Ez. 35:3, 15)

"What shall *we* do?" General Belibni shared a glance with his captain, but the man's eyelids drooped so greatly there where he propped against the wall he mightn't have heard. "Plenty enough," he continued, addressing Tikvah. "First, I must ask, what will *you* do, Jewess?"

"My name is Tikvah, my lord." Unusual boldness drove the correction out of her. This was a cliff's edge she walked, and though Yahweh imbued her with confidence, she must proceed with careful strides.

All three men seemed to agree, if the chambers' abrupt, tension-filled silence gave accurate sign. The general stared at her, brow high.

Kala shifted on his feet, a discreet movement that drew him closer to her side. "Tikvah," he said under his breath in tone of caution.

All she could register, however, was the shape of her name as it formed in her ears, serving as a reminder of the thing she'd at last been granted.

Hope.

Kala's penetrating gaze warmed the side of her face, but she ignored him, unwilling to be lured from the strength she'd discovered in her new, if temporary, position of power.

"As stated, the slave has fire in her," Captain Namtar said, tone drab. So he was listening. Enough to cause her trouble.

But she was not helpless. "The *slave* has the advantage. And thus, the right to a bit of fire." There went her careful strides.

General Belibni tossed out a laugh. "So she does. To all these things."

"Take heed, my lord." Namtar yawned. "Lest that *bit of fire* scorch."

The warning cocked the general's head. "Will you burn me, little Tikvah Jewess?"

If her Lord asked it of her? Without a doubt. As Deborah of old, she would. For what the Babylonians had done to her people, to Yahweh's Holy Temple, Tikvah would drive any number of stakes through this man's unholy temple.

Not that she would say as much. Her newfound boldness had not come with newfound stupidity. God had chosen General Belibni as an instrument of His plan and would extend to him His protection.

As soon as the thought appeared, their reasoning for being there began to solidify in her mind—Belibni wished to use her as entry into the city. Not a terrible plan, but she had a few wishes of her own first.

While she pondered them, while the general waited for an answer she would not voice, Captain Namtar wagged his head to revive himself. He shoved off the wall and crossed to the side table. "We are her much-hated enemy, General. Why would she not?" His fingers coiled around that viper of a whip, and her back muscles spasmed with stinging memory.

At her left, Kala wrapped a firm hand around her forearm, where it hid in the folds of her robe. He gave it a small shake, loosening her fist, which she just then realized had clenched along with her back.

The general's eyes narrowed on the action. "She will not because there is a much-more-hated enemy beyond these four walls."

"She will spit her fire upon us at first opportunity. Is that not true, *Jewess*?" Captain Namtar circled behind her, teeth snapping in her ear, as though he were one of the river beasts from his story bounding into reality. But she had already named him for what he was, a braying ass deserving of no regard. He fought for it just the same, brushing the rolled whip across her shoulders. "I daresay if I expose her flesh, it would bear Zerah's mark."

General Belibni looked on. "Likely, it would bear many."

"Shall we add to them?" The whip stroked down her spine, running over the very marks he hypothesized about.

Kala's grip tightened, but he needn't have feared her response.

A roll of the shoulder twisted her arm out of his grasp. Posture lax, she lifted a dismissive shrug. "Threats will not move me as far as promises."

Interest glossed the general's eyes into shining black pearls. "And where, flame in my hand, do you believe I wish to move you?"

"The city gate. In the quiet of night."

"And I would wish you there because...?" The statement rang of dismissal, but his pearl-eyes glinted, giving him away. He wanted a tool inside Buseyra's walls. Wanted it of her. Badly.

His king had, no doubt, commanded him to take this mountain. The general could either engage in a months-long, tedious siege or use cunning tactics to minimize casualties. At least where his own soldiers were concerned. Tikvah had it from her own *imma's* lips the capacity for slaughter these Babylonians carried in their bones. Oh, the bitter stories her *imma*, her mother, had told.

Obadyah's prediction that Edom would be "cut off by slaughter" was not a concept she struggled to grasp. The Babylonians were adept at slaughter, and was it not the prophet Jeremiah who said destruction would come against the strongholds of Edom like a lion from the floodplain of the Jordan? He could only have meant the lion of Babylon, a prophecy her family had clung to in slavery.

Soon, Tikvah would release that lion upon the Edomites. For when the Lord of Hosts summoned an army to march, when He named an enslaved woman the key that opened the floodgates, there was no commentary. When He said, *Arise ye against her in battle*, there was no criticism. There was only surrender to His will.

On that sobering thought, she spread her hands as if presenting a simple matter. "Why fight your way in when you can walk through the gate?" Though spoken with all the confidence of a steed-mounted general, Tikvah did not know how she might accomplish opening said gate. She would entrust that worry to Yahweh.

"The slave presumes herself a battle strategist," Captain Namtar said behind her, timbre a sardonic drawl.

"As a daughter of God Most High," she shot back, "I presume nothing but obedience to His will."

The step General Belibni took toward her was short but laden with inherent threat. "And what of *my* will? What of obedience to *me*?"

"For the time that your will aligns with His, you have my full obedience and service, General Belibni."

"Pretty speech, and how fluidly it rolls from your mouth. But tell me." Snake-fast, he snatched the tiny parchment from Kala and shook it before her face. "Tell me then, *daughter of a god*. Does this prophecy speak of me and my army? Am I the one who will bring about the foretold destruction of Edom?"

She willed deference into her answer. "When I asked the same, Yahweh gave me two words. Hope. Fulfilled." Granted, He'd given them through another, but Tikvah would not inflict this Babylonian on her vulnerable friend.

The reply eased General Belibni back from before her, but the curl of his lip said it had not satisfied. "Vaguer words could not exist. They might mean anything, and your god uttered them to *you*. So, go on. Inform us. What is this hope of yours, Tikvah the Jewess, god's daughter?"

He snickered, but the continued mockery served only to square her shoulders. Seeming not to notice, he spoke on, avarice glittering in his eyes. "To see Zerah brought to his knees? To hold his tongue in your palm? To watch his house — nay, the entirety of his city! — burn under your flame?"

On the slow lift of one eyebrow, she said, "I daresay, my lord, those are *your* hopes."

"Ha! I will not deny the truth of that. But do you not desire the same? After all, the duke has sorely abused us both."

How casually the Babylonian compared their circumstances. Master Zerah had likely defrauded his yearly tributes to King Nabonidus or committed some other act of treason deserving of severe repercussions. For a fact, he had spoken a spiteful word against his overlord. Many times over. But did the king bear Zerah's scars on his back? Did his general?

Tikvah locked a scoff behind a slash of a smile. "My God will exact justice on my master, Duke Zerah. Does He not promise He will?" She nodded at the scrap dangling before her. "He says nothing, however, of my dearest hope. So, no. I waste no time wishing for those things."

"You lie," Captain Namtar hissed in her ear, breath rank.

She angled away, snorting the potent air from her nostrils. "And you claimed to have only a slingshot to fight off the crocodiles."

"What?" came the captain's abrupt reply, confusion rife in the syllable.

General Belibni, after some moments of blank staring, opened his mouth and bellowed a laugh.

Tikvah and Kala's heads turned in unison for a swap of glances. On his face, her own sentiment reflected at her, though not perfectly. The surprise at Belibni's laughter was there in Kala's wide eyes, but also a modest helping of admiration. *That* she did not share, for what was there to admire about a Hebrew sworn to the service of their enemy?

She narrowed her eyes at him.

He returned her a golden smile that made her cheek prickle with heat.

The moment broke when Captain Namtar came around her front, scowling, eyes bleary from drink. He looked between them, then to his general. "I see not the humor in it."

When General Belibni caught a breath, he pointed at her. "You, woman, are the greatest entertainment I have enjoyed since the month of Adad."

Kala laughed with him, as if reminiscing.

Captain Namtar only slumped. "Must you? I endured the humiliation once already this evening."

"Oh, I must." The general went on speaking to her as if he'd not been interrupted. "Namtar here stormed and swore over losing a bet that earned him a night on a sandbar." On another round laugh, the general gave the captain's shoulder a companionable slap. "Do not hurt your drowned head over the jest, my friend. And leave the woman to me, eh?"

As Namtar shuffled off, scrubbing a hand through his hair, General Belibni turned to her again. "Very well, my blazing flame of a slave. What is *your* hope? What promise do you demand of your lord for this deed done in the night's quiet?"

Her chest expanded as though the hope itself were filling her up, pressing at her ribs to be free, to be spoken and realized. "My hope," she said, unexpectedly breathless, "is to be free, so I might once again see Mount Zion."

Beside her, Kala's indrawn breath blew crisp.

The sound pricked her eyes as she whispered the rest of her heart's longest-held prayer. "I hope to stand witness to the Holy Temple returned to its former glory."

A hush fell over the chamber. Breath passed ragged through Tikvah's constricted throat, but Kala seemed to have frozen his.

Captain Namtar had no trouble speaking. "Ask for the stars, instead. They are easier to reach."

"My captain does not lie. A general's influence over his king goes only so far. I cannot give you but the first."

Tikvah had expected no more than that. "Vow it. Vow to release me with transport and with provender aplenty for the journey to Judah. Vow also to—"

"You want us to turn you loose alone, a lamb in the desert?" Captain Namtar swung his incredulous stare at the general. "We should split her throat now and be done with it. A fitting sacrifice to the god of stupidity."

"I will not be alone." Why must the captain insist on inflicting them with his opinions? She continued, addressing the general. "Yahweh will go before me. And you will free a fellow slave named Shimshon. He will be with me as well."

Kala stepped forward. "This Shimshon fellow, he is your husband? Kin?"

She showed him eyes flat with irritation. "He is an *abba* to me, if you must know."

"We must," the general said. "His trade?"

"He was a shepherd before..." Before Yahweh redirected their lives into slavery and his into mutilation. She cleared her throat. "The wilderness is not unknown to him."

Seeming satisfied with that answer, General Belibni jerked a nod. "Give us aid, and you will receive your freedom from Zerah and from this place."

Tikvah's lashes batted once, twice—relief waylaid by surprise at his prompt agreement. "Shimshon with me?"

"We could hardly release you to your own care," the captain drawled, with irony or sleepiness. Perhaps both, seeing as his eyelids had fallen to slits.

She shook her head. "I would hear the words, General. Vow to release Shimshon and me with our freedom, with transport, and with provender aplenty for the journey to Judah, and I will do whatever lies within my power to give you Busayra."

A wicked grin spread the general's cheeks. "Woman, you are a delight. Is she not, Jew?"

Kala bent his head. "She is, my lord."

Captain Namtar stumbled to the pallet where he threw himself down in a careless flop of limbs. "You should give her to him then." He mumbled into a stack of pillows. "Less hassle than..." The thought dissolved into a snore.

"I will not be *had*," Tikvah said through gritted teeth.

"And yet, my inebriated captain speaks reason." The general resumed the contemplative stroke of his whiskered chin. "Would you like her, boy? In place of the coin? As for the other payment we agreed upon, I would, of course, still supply."

Head swiveling in Kala's direction, Tikvah glared the warning of a woman who had been sold, bought, and exchanged too many times to stand by while arrogant men discussed her value and her fate.

Undeterred, Kala met her head-on, eyes too soft for the hostility she hurled at him, voice too gentle for belief. "Tikvah is beautiful and brave and of the Covenant People, *my* people. I would very much like her...to consider me a friend."

Breath exploded from between her tight lips. With few exceptions, men were alike, no matter their origins. He would not so easily manipulate her. "Remove that lion from your person,"—she gave his breastplate a pointed look—"then shackle yourself to the millstone by the city gate, and I will *consider* it."

"Where is your mercy, woman, your understanding?" The general flung his arm in Kala's direction. "Your *god most high* might have created you for each other. Your courage was certainly formed in the same quick fire."

"Not so, my lord." Kala murmured in that docile tone that rubbed her wrong. "Tikvah outshines me in every way."

She sighed and restrained a roll of the eyes. At least, he wasn't the violent, abusive sort.

"Perhaps, perhaps." Lips twisting, General Belibni crossed his arms, settling in. "We will speak of it again. For now, Tikvah Jewess. Tell me more of this friend you demand accompany you in your freedom. I assume you do not refer to my guard here."

"I do not, General." With a dismissive glance for Kala, she angled toward General Belibni. "My friend is the Hebrew who, come morning, you will find dragging the millstone beside the city gate. And I add he is not to be harmed, not one hair of him, else you lose me as aid."

"Flame in my hand, indeed." General Belibni grinned, much in the way of Namtar's crocodile, all teeth, all threat.

Not directed at her but at those he intended to inflict with her fire, the same he found *entertaining* and *delightful*.

She shuddered anyway. "Well, General of Babylon? Do you concede my demands?"

"I do." He laid a fist to his heart. "For my part, I will grant you and your unharmed friend with freedom, provender, and transport to carry you to Judah. These things for your unquestioning, unflinching service to Babylon in her quest for Edom's destruction."

That last word rang like a bell of doom through Tikvah's brain, rattling her to the bones. Could she manage it? Could she unlock that doom on a city of unsuspecting people?

Throat gone dry, she forced her tongue into the words he wished to hear. "We are agreed."

"Excellent. Now, shall I find you a breastplate to match my liaison's?"

*Scripture referenced: Jeremiah 49:17–19

Chapter 5

*O God, thou art My God; early will I seek thee:
My soul thirsteth for thee, my flesh longeth for
thee in a dry and thirsty land. Because thou
hast been my help, therefore in the shadow of
thy wings will I rejoice. My soul followeth hard
after thee: Thy right hand upholdeth me.* (Ps.
63:1, 8)

Tikvah's cheeks flamed. Several currents of shame
burned through her, but the only one she could
focus on was locked onto her crooked elbow and half-leading,
half-dragging her through the narrow halls in Master Zerah's residence. The echo of Kala's sandals slapping
against the stone walls interrupted the ragged breaths sawing
from her parched throat.

Quiet reigned in the home, and they had naught but
the occasional flickering torch for company. He strode past

each one as he moved in a direct path toward the slave quarters, navigating the place with an intimacy that befuddled her. Had he spent her sequestered time trailing and mapping? He must have, the why of it clearer than the why of his escort to her chambers.

The man remained a mystery, one she feared solving. The hope that he might be of a kindred heart and faith was a too-fragile thing, made weaker by his possessive grip. Was this rough behavior for show? It would be the expectation should a guard or—please, God, no—the master cross their path. Or had the hushed aside he'd shared with the general before leaving the guest chamber been an agreement on *payment*?

Acid roiled in Tikvah's empty stomach. It splashed clear to the back of her tongue when he stopped at the door to the chamber shared by all slaves. A hard swallow forced it back.

Kala nudged her, silent direction for her to stand to the side. He swept an arm through the beaded curtain hanging in the doorway, unsheathed his short sword, and rapped its blade against the torch-less, iron sconce to his right. "Up, the lot of you. Out, *out*." His Akkadian would fly over the heads of most. His commanding tone would not.

From the dark interior, numerous startled cries broke the silence. Within moments, her fellow slaves, still groggy and disoriented, began to emerge. They hurried past her, chins lowered except for two who lifted their gazes, momentarily acknowledging her presence. Mixed emotions played across their faces—confusion, pity, and even disgust.

Nothing ever changed. Except for the courage straightening Tikvah's spine. The Babylonians might not have singled them out as playthings, but neither had Yahweh designated them as instruments of His plan.

The exiled slaves clustered in the hall and awaited orders. Kala continued to peer into the dark, likely tuned to the noises persisting inside.

"Why do you send them away?" she demanded in a brusque whisper.

"For privacy." Arm stretched into the room, he snapped his fingers three times at a shadowed figure. "Move, woman. And you." He turned to those in the corridor. "Leave. Until dawn, I will not permit you to enter again. Be gone, out of doors. Or to the hog pens. I care not where."

Tikvah's stomach sank with dread.

The last to emerge, Sawaha the laundress stormed past, sending a scowl and several strands of beads flying as she went. The moment she'd blended into the departing group, Kala retook Tikvah's elbow and pulled her into the chamber with him. On a clatter of beads, the curtain fell into place behind them.

Despite the window's open shutters, the air smelled rank, a compliment to her mood. Four strides inside, she tugged out of his grip and narrowed him a look rife with suspicion. "What exactly do you plan that requires privacy?"

He spun to her, his large silhouette beginning to form. Faint moonlight glowed through the window at his back, outlining his stiff posture. "Privacy to *speak*, Tikvah." The hurt inflecting his tone clashed with her expectation of anger. "I tell myself it is your ignorance and your hard station that insist on thinking so meanly of me. That you are, in truth, a kind soul. Still, it becomes no less difficult to feel the burn of your scorn. I've done nothing to deserve it."

Tikvah blinked into the murk. His delivery was genuine enough, but that was Babylonian spice tickling her senses. "There will never be a day that armor you wear, along with the king and the gold funding it, will not be deserving of scorn."

"Perhaps, but are we not both doing what we must to survive?" He renewed his patient manner, doing more to soften her heart than his explanations.

Her throat bobbed a dry swallow. "You did not accept the general's offer of payment for me?"

"Not a copper. To wrestle back our portion of our ancestral lands, my kin require every coin the general will give. Every scrap of gold." He raised his forearms before him, letting moonbeams glow in his handsome cuffs.

There, he paused as if to let the concept sink in. It barely had when he turned for the wall niche housing a cold lamp.

"And in this matter of rewards," he continued, almost blithely now, "pay General Belibni no mind. While it would be my pleasure to call one such as yourself my lawful wife, I have no desire to force an arrangement upon you or any other unwilling female."

The strike of flint sprayed sparks over the terracotta lamp. One caught the wick, and light spread across Kala's concentrated features.

He tucked his lighting instrument into a pouch, hooked a finger through the lamp's handle, and turned back to her. Shadows grew around the creases of his frown. "I understand your fear-driven suspicion. But look past the lion on this armor, and you will see I love Hashem with all my heart, with all my soul, and with all my strength, and I have no greater desire than to return to the Land of Promise. I *thirst* for it, Tikvah."

He took a stride toward her, voice tightening with earnest desire. "And when I speak of survival, it is not my own I consider, but that of our people."

He is mine, the Voice whispered, affirming Kala's declaration. *He is your people.*

Kala's heart did appear one with hers. Her eyes crammed shut. *Trust.* Was there anything more difficult to give?

If you cannot trust him, trust me.

Something akin to shame seeped between her ribs to settle like a malaise in her gut. The weight of it drew her chin down. "Forgive me, Kala. I am not accustomed to men who..." Were gentle, honorable. Who did not take without conscience or limit. Especially when attired as the one before her. She would say none of this. "Who regard the ways of Yahweh as sacred."

Breath leaked from her on a long trail. With it went the last from her reservoirs of stamina, the strength that had seen her through the dinner and everything beyond. Legs depleted, she cast about for where to seat herself before her knees gave out.

"You look fatigued. Here." Kala gestured to the nearest pallet.

She accepted with thanks. A woolen blanket, rumpled and still warm, cushioned her ungraceful landing.

"If I recline on another pallet nearby, will you reproach me for wicked intent?" That was a tease in his voice.

She deserved it. Chuckling low, she shook her head. "Please, rest. You should be as weary as I."

"Doubtful. I did not endure the long evening in service to hungry, demanding men." Moving to the bedding opposite, he lowered with a groan to sitting cross-legged. He rubbed a calf, and another quiet groan rolled out of him.

Tikvah folded her legs beneath her, as yet uncertain of his purpose. "Travel up the mountain is no stroll through grassy plains."

It had been nigh on a decade since she'd done it herself, but she well recalled the strain to calves and feet. And not three days hence, every soldier of General Belibni's army would endure it weighed down with armor and weapons and the dread of impending battle.

Nerves struck her stomach and blossomed sweat on her upper lip. So much hinged on her performance. *Too much, too much.*

Nothing is too much for me. To Whom does the battle belong, Daughter?

Tikvah released a trapped breath, head rocking in understanding. She was not alone.

Unaware of her inner turmoil, Kala unstrapped a sandal to expose a dusty foot. "The day has indeed been long and toilsome. But it has ended…"

"Without bloodshed?" Her own, specifically. The general had already assured her he would warn Master Zerah away from discipline, but General Belibni could not control what transpired after he left come morning. And as far as the master would know, the general would have no reason to return within the period it took for bruises to fade.

"There is still opportunity for that. Should I misbehave." Peering up from his second sandal, Kala sprouted a sudden grin. "The general advises I guard against a certain sharp tongue."

Her blurt of laughter rent the stillness of the night. "You are safe from that, soldier. For now."

"Do not spare me too long. My sister tells me I am a better man when subjected to a woman's occasional sermoning."

"She sounds wise."

Smile growing, he brushed red dust from an ankle. "Remind me never to allow the two of you together in the same tent." He spoke as though such a situation were a genuine possibility.

As though Tikvah's entire existence was not hanging in the balance, to be decided by her own questionable prowess. As though her long-prayed-for hope had a real chance of becoming a reality.

The laughter that left her this time tumbled out choppy and stiff, rife with doubt. He glanced up from rubbing a foot where he'd balanced it on the opposite knee.

She hurried to speak first. "I worry about the others out in the cold."

"They will survive. Besides,"—he returned his foot to the ground more forcefully than necessary—"they deserve a bit of discomfort."

Was there a story behind that? She cocked him a brow in question.

He obliged. "While I waited for my lord to finish dining, I heard the serving slaves whispering, speaking ill of you. And while I toured the grounds, more of the same came from this very chamber. If any of that bitter lot did not speak a word against you, I did not encounter them."

Tikvah sighed and rose, then went to the pitcher and basin by the door. Pleased to find water reflecting high in the vessel's neck, she collected both, as well as the damp washing cloth beside, and began back. "I can well imagine what they were saying, that I'd brought all this on myself. That I *deserve* whatever comes my way." Lowering to her knees before him, she set the items on the floor and lifted a smile, meager though it was. "Nothing you heard is new. But...thank you."

It had been a long, lonely while since anyone had stood up for her. Rather, anyone with the power to do something about it. She tapped his big toe, then hoisted the pitcher.

After a moment's hesitation, wherein he stared at her in perplexity, he settled his foot in the basin. "The general was correct. You have an extraordinary courage."

She suspended the pitcher on its forward tilt above his foot so she could meet his gaze. She could not have him misunderstanding the situation. "Do not praise me, Kala. You see only what our God gives me for this purpose."

"Then praise His holy name."

"Omein."

Water poured from her pitcher's spout. The dust and grime darkening his skin surrendered to the water's flow, and Tikvah envisioned this life of hers washing away in the same manner.

General Belibni with his army would storm the mountain. Flames would consume every structure. And Tikvah, Shimshon with her, would be free.

Free.

Could it be possible, that freedom? Or would pursuing it, dreaming of it, lead only to heartache and punishment? Should he get his claws into her, Master Zerah would show no mercy.

Rather fond of her tongue, she swallowed with difficulty, then fisted the cloth and began scrubbing the top of Kala's foot. "You...go to Judah?"

Try as she might, she could not halt the forming notion that he might consider taking them with him. Not a terrible prospect. Travel to their ancestral home with Kala? Her pulse fluttered, and to her horror, she realized it was not the first part of the thought that caused the palpitation, but the last. Before she could ponder the irrationality of that, he spoke.

"We do. Myself and two other men, our families besides. We are scholars trained in the arts of war. Selected as aids for this campaign. As need arises, we translate or serve as liaisons." He patted the empty scabbard lying along his thigh. "I can fight, same as any other foot soldier, but General Belibni keeps us at the rear guard. Our value is not in our swords, but in our minds."

"And for payment?"

"Freedom from Babylon. Passage to Judah. Funds to reestablish ourselves." He paused, tone softening. "Same as you."

The swab of her cloth, gentler now, slowed to a crawl. She couldn't help the hopeful lift of her sight, but though her lips parted, her closing throat could not form the thoughts screaming in her mind. *Take me, take us with you!* Air wheezed out of her. Then he took her dripping hand in his and spoke, cutting off her breath altogether.

"You and Shimshon would be most welcome to join our band."

"I..." The ache around her voice box multiplied to unbearable levels, so that her next words emerged hoarse. "We would like that. Very much."

He enclosed her trembling hand in his other, lips curving inside his beard. "As would I." Had his voice gone hoarse too? No, that couldn't be.

Pulling from his hold, she resumed work by guiding his wet foot from the basin. She used the edge of her robe to pat the drips from his heel. "Your family, they would not mind?"

"My imma would delight in it. My brother will as well, for you will offer another ear for his chattering wife, and she will be glad for help at the hand mill."

"You have no wife?" Head bent, she squeezed her eyes shut. *Impertinent, woman!* This man was a stranger, a questionable one at that. Was she so desperate for a guardian, she'd look twice at the first male to show her kindness?

"None yet."

The sound of trickling of water blinked her lashes open. He'd switched feet and was pouring fresh water over his wiggling toes. The sight sent a chortle to her nose.

She looked up to find him grinning. Her shoulders eased down, and following his lead, she twisted her lips and flicked a finger at his chest. "Have you found none who will abide that lion on your chest?"

"Oy." Feigning offense, he laid a hand over the stamped leather. In the next breath, he let it fall, along with his smile. When he set the pitcher aside, its *thunk* against the ground seemed the establishing of a cornerstone. "I've found none who match my passion to reestablish in Judah. Life in Babylon suits many too well, but I will not settle for scraps. I am Kala ben Mahlon, and I will know our homeland."

His deep voice resonated through the chamber. Through Tikvah as well. How could it not? He spoke her very heart. The knot in her throat that had just begun to relax tightened again. Terrible timing, for she must respond to that.

Unable for long moments to bear the accumulating pain, she could only gather water in the cup of her palm and bathe his foot. Abounding in patience, he kept silent as she ministered to him, each stroke of her cloth then her robe a gesture of gratitude.

At last, having recovered her voice, she removed the basin to the side and bowed her head with all the humility of her enslaved status. "I have misjudged you, Kala ben Mahlon, and for that I must beg forgiveness."

"Not so," he was quick to say. "You have earned your distrust, your anger."

"And yet, my conscience pricks." Yahweh forgive her, she should have trusted *Him*.

"Peace, Tikvah." Kala's long, brown fingers appeared in her lowered vision. They extended in offering.

She slipped hers over his calloused palm and felt the connection in her marrow. To him. To their shared dream. To their people.

When they curled their fingers to solidify the hold, her mouth spread in a smile that matched his. "Shalom, my friend."

Chapter 6

Hashem shall roar from on high, and utter his voice from his holy habitation. (Jer. 25:30)

Something roused Tikvah from a dreamless sleep. A noise. She stirred and listened.

It came again, a low-timbred murmur, that of a man. As if at his prayers.

Who among us ever prayed at this hour? None she could recall.

Then, an image of Kala's sun-kissed face sifted through Tikvah's foggy mind. Her eyes cracked open.

Diffuse light filtered through the chamber. Not yet the bright rays of dawn, this light came with the gray mists that rolled over the distant peaks.

A bend in her stiff neck brought Kala into her vision. He stood before the wide-open arched window. Its broad, stone sill, low enough to sit upon, pressed against his upper thighs.

The windowsill had witnessed numerous slaves surrendering themselves by leaping over it. Tikvah, thank Yahweh, had never succumbed to such a profound sense of hopelessness. And now, as she observed Kala assuming a posture of prayer—his head covered with a kerchief, face uplifted, and hands open before him—she understood why.

The Lord God had preserved her, along with His servant at the mill, for this day. He had saved her for this morning when she gazed upon their very own Moshe, come to lead them out of slavery, through the wilderness, and into the Promised Land.

For hadn't they been promised as much?

For their violence against Judah and against her, Edom would receive God's wrath, unsavory business though it was. Jacob's house would regain possession. That started with her, with Shimshon, with Kala and his kin.

On cue, a bright orange beam streaked through the gloom. Its brilliance flashed across the sky, transforming nebulous gray into pale blue. Awe and gratitude swelled within Tikvah and threatened to pour from her throat on a song of redemption.

Smiling sleepily, she held it in check. Yahweh had gifted her with many things. A songbird's voice was not among them.

How tragic it would be to startle her *very own Moshe* and lose him over the window's ledge?

She chose instead to push herself upright, tuck upraised knees under interlocked arms, and watch the birth of a new day.

If she also happened to steal lingering glimpses of a certain handsome man at his prayers, well, who would blame her? Not the Lord, who had without question placed that man in her path. Nor the man himself, who had without hesitation placed himself in her life.

Kala had left no thread of doubt that once they were free of this mission, she would fall under his authority and protection. He would make it so. The warm, lingering glances he'd dispensed above the gentle curve of his mouth made *other* promises he could not possibly mean after so short an acquaintance.

At each instance, Tikvah lowered her lashes in confusion, but by the time the lamp's wick sent up a curl of smoke and winked out, she admitted to herself she did not like hiding from him, not even her gaze.

Now, properly rested and clear-headed, she concluded that the night's enchantment had disoriented her, made her imagine things. Even so, as she watched him beseech their God, she decided one other thing: the man she'd been so ready to distrust only hours before would, in fact, make an excellent spouse.

The mutter of his prayers faded into a chest-filling breath. On the exhale, he scrubbed the back of his wrist across his cheek and sniffed.

Though loath to intrude on his meditations, she recognized that time was fleeting. Noises from the house were already echoing down the corridor. Soon, someone would barge in with demands of them both.

She rose and, straightening her garment as she walked, padded up behind him. *"Boker tov."* The Hebrew words, though rusty from sleep, flowed up from her soul.

Passing her a smile to match the sunrise, Kala spoke their traditional reply of, *"Boker."* He took in her responding smile before stepping left so she might join him at the window.

Good morning light, she'd said, and never had the traditional greeting been more exact.

The color of a ripe date, the sun peeked its upper curve over the valley floor. Rays fanned out above it, heralding the glory of God. The sheer drop beyond the window only enhanced the sight's terrible splendor.

Had the light reached Yerushalayim yet? Did the remnant who'd been left behind perceive how the Lord worked His perfect will on the heights of Edom? Could they feel His retribution advancing on their betrayers?

Whatever came of this fulfillment of prophecy would be no reckoning of their greatest enemy and oppressor, Babylon, but it was a fine start.

Unbidden, her gaze skipped to the lion stamped on Kala's armor. Up on hind legs, it clawed the air, mouth open in a silent roar that shook all the known world.

"Have you seen her? Judah?" Kala's question wrenched her gaze up.

Had she not told him as much in the night? She scrolled back through their long conversation but encountered only discussions of the prophet's message. He'd shared other passages from Jeremiah and Ezekiel, names with which she was familiar.

They'd far from exhausted the topic by the time sleep claimed her. She did not recall deciding to close her eyes. So much left to learn of one another, of their people's traditions, prophecies, future...

"I have. My abba is a poor vinedresser in the hills of Galilee." She smiled, pleased to speak of it with someone who cared. "After the fall, General Nebuzzaradan left him and my imma behind, along with others to tend the land."

"What of Johanan's rebellion? How did they escape it?"

"They didn't. When Johanan moved through Judah preaching refuge in Egypt, my parents protested, choosing to believe Jeremiah's message instead. It didn't matter. They were very young—younger than myself now—and hadn't the strength or resources to resist. Johanan forced them to leave along with the rest."

"But they returned."

"Yes. They were of the handful to escape when Babylon's sword found them there."

King Nebuchadnezzar had not been content to destroy Judah. His legions had marched next into Egypt, and all those who'd believed themselves safe there were slaughtered as Jeremiah had foretold.

"It was before my day." Tikvah sighed. "But my imma believes Yahweh noted their faith in Him and His prophet. And so, they were spared and able to return to Judah."

"Your family has a long and noble history of faith. How then, did you end up here?"

How else but through Edomite bitterness and cruelty? "My parents arrived back on their lands only to find it overtaken by Edomites. Before they could make a case for themselves, they were enslaved. Allowed to stay on and work the land but forced to surrender all profit to the Edomite lord who'd moved in. I arrived a few years later."

"Edom is a far trek from the hills of Judah."

"Too far." Tikvah focused far across the land, looking as northerly as the window allowed, the closest she ever came to seeing her homeland. She kept her voice light as she expounded. "Our Edomite master was a relentless gambler. Every year, one or two of my family and neighbors were carted off to distant lands. Sold to pay off debts, as I was."

Kala allowed a pause, as if in respectful silence, before proceeding. "How old were you?"

"Old enough to remember the lush fields, the scent of sage warming in the morning sun, the bleat of newborn lambs echoing through the hills." Eyelids drifting downward, she inhaled, trying to recall the scents and sounds, but all she picked up were the high whistle of wind, the slight scorch of flat cakes cooking on heated stone, and the tangy spice that drifted about Kala's person. She clung to the last.

"What else?" His urgency drew her eyes open. The man held himself tightly, expectantly.

She knew what he wanted to hear. Knew also that, once he did, the truth would grieve him. But she would not deny him that. "I remember Yerushalayim."

"Tell me of it. Does anything remain of the City of Holiness?"

Last Tikvah saw, it was little more than a city of carnage. The faithful few who occupied surrounding lands held the ruins sacred, but thirty-six years had passed since the siege and invasion, and none, not even the Edomite rats that infested their lands, had made repairs. Did they find the task too overwhelming, or did Yahweh prevent it? It had been He, after all, who'd permitted its desolation. When would He authorize its restoration?

She had no answer, yet Kala waited for news, for some word of encouragement.

His bearing reverent, he looked deep into her eyes, as if they'd been blessed for having seen the Holy Land, and he wished a portion of it on himself.

What to tell him? What hope might be found in a jumble of broken stone?

A shrug lifted her shoulder. "I saw it only from a distance." It stood on a mount, outlined against a storm-darkened sky. They'd passed it on their way to and from an uncle's home west of the city. She had been quite young, but the vision had stamped itself in her mind.

"And? What was there?"

There was no lying and no help for the truth. "Nothing, Kala. Crumbled walls. A mound of scorched rubble."

"Ah..." His frame flagged. "And yet you long to see it again."

Ever so much. "Yerushalayim," she began, a passage from the Book of Kings, one of the few she remembered, coming to her lips almost unbidden, "the city which I have chosen for Me to put My name there." Her sight drifted to that lion, sadness consuming her as it had the day she'd taken in the destruction and wept.

Though tears did not sting, her tightening throat scratched with her next question. "Whose name is there now?"

"Whose do you think, Tikvah?" Before she could answer, Kala continued, voice firming. "Hashem shall roar from on high and utter His voice from His holy habitation; He shall mightily roar upon His habitation. And the peaceable habitations are cut down because of the fierce anger of Hashem." A smile grew upon him. "The word of Hashem to the prophet Jeremiah. And to us."

The words circled her heart and entered with a resounding note of Truth. The prophet Jeremiah was a man of their day, having lived during her lifetime. He'd voiced his message for her.

Mightily roar... Fierce anger of Hashem... Upon His habitation.

Yahweh had not abandoned His covenant people, not even for a moment. Tikvah never doubted, not really. But, at times, her anger toward the desecration and those who'd performed it ran too hot for reason.

Ducking her head, Tikvah murmured agreement. "It is a good word." As she'd told Kala in the night, she remembered a few passages from one of the last great prophets. This was not one of them. She could have used it in years past to buoy her faith. She could use it now. "Will you speak it again?"

He did, ending on a triumphant grin. "I fight not for the lion of Babylon, Tikvah." He rapped a finger against his breastplate. "But for the Lion of Judah. He stalks from His den on high, my friend, and soon,"—he canted toward her, eyes lit with passion—"we shall hear His roar."

At the proclamation, a fire flashed through her veins, heating them with anticipation. The man's zeal was catching, the burn of his eyes bright and eager for battle. He was handsome, no denying, all the more so for the pure and noble heart that beat within him.

Did Joshua and David look like this before cleansing the land of evil? Were these the words they might have spoken to rouse their troops, to bring praise to Yahweh before the battle shofar sounded?

Tears sprouted, reducing Tikvah to a rapid series of nods. "Soon," she eked out and met Kala quote for quote. "Then, upon Mount Zion shall be deliverance, and there shall be holiness." She paused there. Would he recall the next part?

The man picked right up, proving why he'd been selected for this mission. "And the house of Jacob shall possess their possessions."

She exhaled a laugh. "Well done. I see now why King Nabonidus selected you." He hadn't read the prophecy more than a few times, and already he'd locked it into his heart and mind.

He seemed not to hear the compliment as he launched into another quote. "'For, lo, the days are coming, saith Hashem to Jeremiah, that I will bring back from captivity my people Israel and Judah, and I will cause them to return to the land that I gave to their fathers, and they shall possess it. Houses and fields and vineyards shall be possessed again in this land.'"

Did he mean *their* abbas? Might it mean *them*? "O, Lord, may it be so," she breathed.

Kala's gaze shot behind her. "Tikvah," he whispered with sudden urgency. "Ready yourself."

The crash of beads cut short any reply. She twisted toward the clatter.

Her heart gave a single alarming thud. She'd expected a slave, but Master Zerah's rotund, sweating form filled the entry. The scowl on his face vanished upon sight of Kala.

Tikvah saw no more, for her diligent guard stepped forward and one pace left, placing himself before her.

"Pardon, young soldier," Master Zerah said, somewhat stiff. "I did not realize you were here."

Though Kala held his hands at his lower back in a harmless position, he'd curled them into hard balls. The outline of taut muscle ran the length of his arms, and the delicate cuffs bit into the flesh of his forearms. "Duke Zerah," was all he gave the man for reply.

"I come inquiring about my slaves. Why do they stand in a shivering gaggle outside the stables, and why does this one remain abed?"

"*This one* remains under my protection. The why of it you will have to learn of my lord, General Belibni."

"What will the duke learn of me?" The general's gruff voice lured her sight around Kala's rigid frame.

Master Zerah, whose shoulders bounced to his ears, spun and clasped his hands before his paunch. As the general swept aside the beads and stalked into the chamber, Master Zerah shuffled backward, bowing as he went. "Ah! My most gracious lord, how have you risen this fine morning? I trust you slept—"

"How fares our king's newest amusement?" The general spoke over Master Zerah's platitudes. He looked beyond the man to Kala, eyebrow raised in query. Behind him, Captain Namtar pushed through the beads without bothering to shove them aside. His hair stood on end, and his jaw stretched wide with a massive yawn.

Master Zerah's spine snapped straight. "Newest amuse... D-do you mean—"

"She is rested and well, General," Kala answered his superior, setting her heart at an irregular rhythm.

He said nothing they had not rehearsed. Still, the words sapped the strength from her knees and made the room spin. She gripped the back of Kala's tunic.

He shifted into her touch, obliterating any shame at her forward behavior.

"B-but, your lordship!" Master Zerah spluttered. "You would give the king a despoiled woman?"

"Myself?" General Belibni laid a hand across his chest. "His Majesty does not receive the gift of the woman from *my* hand, Duke, but from yours."

"I, well, that was not what I—"

"Besides, not a man here touched her in the night. And because I can assume you would not have given me a despoiled woman yourself, she must be as fit for the king's chamber as the next maiden."

"Certainly. But her scars!"

Belibni waved that off. "Bah. Scars are a token of strength. They will amuse His Majesty, for he is well aware of your exceptional cruelty." While Master Zerah spluttered on, the general continued. "On behalf of Nabonidus, King of the Four Corners of the World, I thank you for the present of a splendid slave. Should he be pleased enough, she will make a striking addition to his harem. And perhaps, just perhaps, if she is feeling generous, she will speak on your behalf before His Majesty."

"Doubtful," Captain Namtar contributed on a mutter. He picked at his nails. "But you can always pray. Where it concerns the king, the gods know you could use the help."

A smirk slid over General Belibni's mouth, but he did not contradict his captain.

In fact, a quiet settled over the men so profound that Master Zerah's bobbing throat clicked. "Naturally, I offer only my best to..." His neck jutted forward in a spasm, much like a vulture downing a too-large bite. "To His Exalted Majesty."

"Wise," the general said through a whetted smile. "I cannot take the slave with me at present. Keep her in safety until I return four days hence to conclude our talks. In my absence, do refrain your tempter, Zerah. It would displease me to find her in fresh marks."

Pallor washed over the master's face. "She shall be safe as a lamb in the stall, Qos love her, as well tended as—"

"Excellent." General Belibni slapped her master's shoulder, sending him stumbling forward.

Before Master Zerah could regain his footing, the general marched out. He disappeared in seconds, leaving only the sound of beads swinging and boots tapping on flagstone.

Grunting and grumbling, Master Zerah rubbed his shoulder.

"And, by all the gods in the heavens," Captain Namtar said with a curl of the lip directed Tikvah's way, "give the slave some decent food. She's dreadfully thin." On that complementary note, he went the way of his general, Master Zerah hot on his heels, blubbering offers of the best cucumbers and olives to break their fast.

Kala didn't move, and Tikvah didn't breathe until the bead curtain had ceased its dance. Only then did her breath explode outward and her shoulders descend from their tense perch.

Every word had been a charade. Just the same, it unsettled her no end.

Tenderness softened Kala's face as he turned to her with an extended hand. He caught himself short and lowered it with an apologetic dip of the lashes. "This danger we place upon you churns my gut."

Laughter stuttered out of her, more nerves than anything, though she'd been shooting for dismissal. "You give yourself too much credit, soldier. Yahweh alone places me in danger, and Yahweh alone will see me through it." In whatever form that might come. "I am honored to be His servant and yours."

"Tikvah…" He stepped nearer, voice lowering into the realm of intimate. "Once we have accomplished our mission here—"

"Kala! We leave!" The captain's voice boomed down the corridor, wrenching Kala's neck toward it.

Swinging back to her, Kala sighed. Unspoken words hung between them, but neither time nor duty allowed them a voice.

One thing was certain. He would leave her now.

Fear gripped her. Clinging to Yahweh's promise, she stomped it into submission but could not eradicate the tremble in her whisper. "You must take your leave."

"So I must," he said, as reluctant as she. However, when he leaned forward, quite close, there was nothing reluctant about him. Warmth brushed her ear when he next spoke. "Shalom, Tikvah. God bless you and keep you."

The prayer, or perhaps the man, bound up the wind in her throat. She held herself still until a nudge at her clenched fingers opened them for the tiny, crimped scroll he pressed against her palm.

Then he was gone, leaving her in a lovely cloud of his Babylonian spice.

*Scripture quoted and referenced: Jeremiah 30:3; 32:15; 43–44; 1 Kings 11:36

Chapter 7

For the day of the Lord is near upon all the heathen: as thou hast done, it shall be done unto thee: thy reward shall return upon thine own head. (Obad. 15)

The miller's dogs were alerted to Tikvah's arrival before the side gate squealed under her shove. Tails high and wagging, they darted past Shimshon where he used methodical strokes to scrape a straw broom over the tiles around the grinding stone. He dropped the broom and turned, seeming to follow their growls as the two play-battled each other to reach her first.

Shimshon came right behind them, strides sure. His shoulders were set more squared in his hunched back than she'd seen since last winter when the miller's wife went away on an extended stay in the valley to tend her sick sister. "Eeh-ah," he called ahead of himself.

She would have thought the blurt a reprimand if she didn't know him incapable of any harshness. That was relief, plain and proper, driving him toward her at imprudent speed. If he did not take care, he would trip over a dog.

"Forgive my tardiness, abba." Ignoring the beasts circling her legs, she threw an arm around Shimshon's neck and squeezed hard. "As well as my paltry offerings." She pulled back to press a scrap of flat bread into his hand. "This was all I found in—"

He batted it away, then found her mouth with a rapping finger and made noises of demand—for an explanation, if she was not mistaken.

"Did you think I had forgotten you? Never."

He shook his head and pantomimed the lash of a whip.

"Ah, no, fear not. I am unharmed." A starched laugh escaped her. "Though I confess I did earn myself a flogging and more. But by Yahweh's grace, I received instead a blessing beyond imagining. We both did, abba! Come, come. Eat while I tell you."

This time, when she tapped his hand with the rolled scrap—all she'd been able to rustle up in the banquet-ravaged kitchen—he wrapped calloused fingers around it. He grunted his version of a prayer of thanks as he dug his teeth into the bread, then ripped off a chunk.

Tikvah took him by the elbow and squinted against the sun angling down. "The day's heat is already upon us.

Shall we sit against the wall?" At his nod, she began
toward the deep shadows sheltering at the base of the
courtyard wall.

On a typical morning, by this hour, Shimshon would
have already taken a hundred turns about the mill's axis.
Today, he alone occupied the yard. Even the donkey was
absent, probably suffering the strikes of its master's im-
perious heel. Miller Reuel was not known for a gentle
touch.

But why would he be out so early? The taverns would
yet be closed. That left curiosity over the visiting Babylonians and hope of a glimpse as they departed the city.

General Belibni's presence had scrambled the entire
city, starting at the main gate. Their soldiers manned it
and would allow none to pass through while the general
was unarmed inside Master Zerah's home. All business
must wait until they left, an event that would transpire
in moments, judging by the clatter of hooves against
packed earth.

Few horses lived in Busayra; the heights were not
ideal for sustaining them. Thus, the approaching pro-
cession could be none other than the general and his
small entourage. Kala should be among them.

Face turned that way, Tikvah resisted the urge to run
to the courtyard's main gate and press her cheek to the
wood on the chance she might spot him through the slats.
Scoffing softly through her nose, she carried on toward the

wall. She would be no gawking miller. Although she had every reason and right to see the man off.

Once she'd settled Shimshon on the ground in the shade and shooed the dogs away, she started in on a summary of what had transpired since she'd seen him last. Was it only yesterday morning?

No time for that wonder. She dismissed it and scooted close, lowering her voice to an excited whisper. "They were three at the master's house. The general—Belibni, he is called—a Captain Namtar, who is a dull-witted pebble in my sandal, and a foot soldier named Kala." She spoke the last with irrepressible reverence, but she doubted that was the reason Shimshon's jaw halted mid-chew.

Another laugh bubbled out of her. "You appreciated his name quicker than I. Yes, my keen friend, Kala is Hebrew, a loyal servant of Yahweh. There is much to tell! But I must be brief."

The increasing racket from the city gate warned that patrons would arrive shortly.

She clipped her volume to a shred of a whisper. "The general has enlisted my services, Shimshon. If I perform with faith, I will earn our freedom. Freedom! Imagine it. Once the city is under Babylonian control, they will grant us that plus provisions and transport to Judah."

Breath passed rapidly through her broad smile as she waited for his wordless exclamation, for a shout of joy, for anything other than a single thoughtful nod. "To Judah, abba! Did you not hear?"

He signaled to proceed with a quick nod and hand swirl. Was he in shock? Or perhaps, listening for affirmation with that ear he had always cocked toward the Lord.

"In two nights' time," she continued, unperturbed, "when the moon is at its darkest, I am to find my way to Master Zerah's cellar. In it there is an old, forgotten entry covered by a great stone. From what they tell me, it opens to a goat path that trails down to the valley." So much cleverer than the city gate in the quiet of night.

Shimshon parted his mouth for a series of increasingly animated mutterings.

"You see the plan, yes? It is simple. Or should be, except I have just come from there. Large amphorae block all but the stone's top curve. Four of them sit in a rack. Their seals are unbroken, so they will be quite heavy."

During her speech, Shimshon's pitch had grown excited, emphasized at the end by a rapid slap to his chest. He would move the barrels, those chest-slaps said.

Caught by his fever, she gripped his hand. "I had so hoped you would offer. So, on the way here, I devised a plan to get you into the master's house."

His noises cut off, an uneasy stillness coming over him. Shimshon had not been to the master's house since the day they took his eyes, but no matter the nightmare memories, this would not daunt him. She would not allow it. Especially considering what all would be required of the man.

"As the Lord lives, who made our very souls and who has called us to this purpose, I will not let them touch you." For what else could they take but his life? And that they would not do.

Though his lips paled, Shimshon waited in patient, unflinching silence for her to continue.

Drawing a deep breath, she did. "How do you feel about playing sick?"

Chapter 8

And the Lord, he it is that doth go before thee; he will be with thee, he will not fail thee, neither forsake thee: fear not, neither be dismayed. (Deuteronomy 31:8)

On the prescribed evening, Tikvah knelt beside a scowling Shimshon, waiting for him to return the bowl to his lips. The one slurp would not suffice. "Best to eat it all," she coaxed. "I used the same dose as Matron Houda when her boy chewed those oleander leaves. Do you recall? It was some time ago now, but I watched her prepare the purgative. She did not dilute hers but poured it straight down the child's gullet." Then darted off as he spewed.

As though Tikvah had served Shimshon the outcome of that emetic—instead of a savory soup—he wrinkled his nose at the dish cradled between his palms.

He could not back out now. He could not. Before the sliver of that night's moon crested the sky, Kala would be at the cellar's hidden entry, scores of Babylonian soldiers behind him.

But what she asked of Shimshon was no trifling thing, either. She laid a supportive hand on his shoulder. "It is not the most agreeable plan, I admit. If you have another..." She let her voice drag, providing space for him to insert another suggestion.

On a heave of breath, he wagged his head. Resolve firmed, he raised the bowl, set it against his mouth, and tipped. His throat lurched four times before he lowered the empty dish and wiped his sleeve across dripping lips.

Eyes wide, Tikvah took the bowl and set it aside. "Well. That is done then. You make a true sacrifice, abba."

In reply, Shimshon bent to drag a finger through the dirt. The single word he formed was almost illegible, but Tikvah would recognize it in any condition. A wild blush warmed her cheeks, and she shamed herself with gratitude Shimshon did not witness it.

He watched her now through a cocked ear. Could he hear the escalated rhythm of her heart?

She wiggled, becoming uncomfortable. "You...wish to know of our new benefactor?" At Shimshon's nod, she fumbled for what to share.

She and Kala had had been blessed with one night to acquaint themselves and hardly that. Only half a night, truth told, by the time they'd been alone to learn anything of value.

Surely, though, she had something interesting to share and pass the time. Something that would not give away the girlish patter of her heart. "In the short while we spoke, I gleaned that he is a foot soldier acting as personal guard to General Belibni. Or perhaps he truly is the general's guard? Whichever the case, his appointment is as...what did he call it?" Her gaze drifted to the pen where the donkey munched hay. "Liaison, it was. Of the secret sort. A spy, if you will. He is an expert in our region's language and culture and is proficient in several tongues."

Head lowered, she twisted the end of her waist sash about a finger and thought on those handsome honey-colored eyes of his and how they spoke a language all their own. He seemed rather proficient in that, too. But what did she know of the ways of a man toward a woman? Only that this man displayed kindness and bravery, as well as loyalty to the God of Abraham.

A poke to her arm sent her jumping. Shimshon's sightless stare demanded she continue.

She cleared her throat and unwound the fabric from her blue-tipped finger. "There is little more to say. After we finish this unsavory business, I suppose we shall both get to know him better. I cannot recall much more."

Shimshon snorted with his entire chest. If he had eyes, he could not express his disbelief more clearly.

She bopped him with her sash. "Very well. If you insist, I will say more on the matter of Kala the Liaison." Ignoring Shimshon's snort of laughter, she proceeded. "He is tall. A head above myself if not more, and for a woman, I have quite the stature. He is also strong."

At the curious tip of Shimshon's head, she added, "I have no way to judge, naturally, for he only stood guard against the far wall, but I did see..." The swell of his arms beneath his tunic and the definition of his muscular calves. "...the armor he wore. I imagine wearing such heavy equipment would require great strength."

Head thrown back, Shimshon bellowed a laugh, then pulled her in for a fumbling kiss to the top of her head.

Beaming, she soaked it in. It wasn't as if he never showed affection, but this gesture felt different. Like a celebration. Like Passover, Shavuot, and the Festival of Booths rolled into one. This kiss, this breezy laughter, was an acknowledgment of a possible future, one that did not include chains or whips or grinding stones.

In a burst of hope-filled joy, Tikvah threw her arms around Shimshon and mashed her lips to his leathery cheek, then took the opportunity to whisper a secret in his ear. "Our Kala is quite handsome, too."

Our? A living thing, the word had leaped off her tongue of its own accord. But now that it was out and free, she would not wish it back. Kala was indeed theirs.

Their people. Their Caleb, the spy. Their *very own Moshe*.

Shimshon returned her embrace, arms trembling with emotion. Or was that...

He froze, then groaned.

Tikvah released him as she might a sun-scorched stone.

Gripping his stomach, he loosed another low moan. Sweat exploded across his forehead.

At the sight, instant remorse set in. "Oh, my dear abba. Forgive me."

Arms wrapped tight about his middle, he shook his head and rocked.

Lord of Hosts, see him through, I pray. See us to the end of this night and far beyond.

As if in answer, the door to the miller's house squealed open. Miller Reuel, wrapped in his finest blue linens, began down the curving stairs. Yahweh's timing was indeed perfect.

Tikvah hurried to throw an arm around Shimshon's shoulders and murmur, "Are you ready? Miller Reuel has appeared on the stair. He looks our way."

With a vigorous nod, Shimshon opened his mouth for a resounding groan. The proportion of theater to actual misery was unclear, but it aided their charade.

Tikvah waited until the miller reached the last tread before raising her voice to say, "Up, now, up," and hauling Shimshon to his feet. He floundered convincingly and leaned into her, body stiff and bent with pain. They stumbled toward the small rear gate that led into the back alley. Tikvah's usual entry point.

"What is that slave's problem?" the miller called, the boom of his voice reverberating through the courtyard.

Shimshon's feet stuttered, but Tikvah would not let him pause. Neither did she afford the miller a glance. "He is most ill, Miller Reuel. I must take him—"

"Lies," the man spat. His sandals slapped the ground as he bustled his portly frame toward them. "He pretends illness to avoid work. Enough, you lazy mule. Return to—"

Without warning, Shimshon convulsed and spewed onto the square of ground between them.

The man's shriek rent the air. He scrambled back, skipping and hopping. "My sandals, you disgusting animal! You have ruined them!"

"On the morrow, I will clean them," Tikvah soothed while ushering Shimshon back into motion. He'd not ceased convulsing. "But for now, Shimshon requires watchful nursing under warm shelter. Since such cannot be found here, I take him to our master's house. If I did otherwise he would be displeased."

Then he would come after the miller for payment, for a slave on lease must not suffer permanent harm.

Miller Reuel kicked off a sandal. "Yes, by Qos on high, take the wretch. Go, go!"

"As you say."

Tikvah urged Shimshon forward, and they shuffled off again. At the gate, she stopped by the water jar to draw up a dipper. He swished, spat, and gulped, but before they'd gone ten paces, he brought that swallow up again. Bent double, he wet the packed dirt.

"Oi." Tikvah patted his back. "My poor friend. Shall we rest?" Even as she asked, she looked ahead down the narrow alley and calculated how long it would take to reach home at this pace.

They must make it back before the master finished dining, or they chanced running into house slaves engaged in serving the evening repast. And she did not wish to encounter Aos on the best of occasions. Never mind with Shimshon in tow.

Shimshon knew as much and must have weighed his discomfort against the risk, for he straightened, hooked Tikvah's hand about his elbow, and pressed on.

Since that day long ago when Shimshon lost so much and followed it up with praise to the Almighty, there had never been a moment Tikvah had not loved and admired the man for his astounding faith and courage. This day, as he trekked the back streets of Busayra without faltering, he did not spoil that admirable pattern.

Tikvah kept them to the deepening shadows, all the while sweating in the evening chill, worrying she'd given him too strong a dose. Had Mistress Houda's boy heaved so continually, so violently? Tikvah did not recall such sickness.

Fear pooled in her gut, increasing with each step that took them closer to the house. Agitated, disjointed prayers scattered through her mind. It would take an almighty God to make anything out of them. Fortunately, Yahweh was just that.

Trust. Trust Him, Tikvah. He will not fail you.

At last, they hurried through the rear slaves' entrance, Tikvah whispering guidance. "Two paces more, then left. One step down. Watch your head. The entry is low. That's it. Almost there." That they'd made it thus far without passing a single individual was a miracle in itself. Buoyed by that realization, Tikvah allowed herself a deep breath.

Too soon. For in the next moment, Sawaha entered from the laundry courtyard, a pile of stiff garments stacked in a basket on her hip. Her dark eyes landed first on Tikvah but shifted to Shimshon, where they lingered and narrowed.

Shimshon drooped. His weight, lean as it was, settled against Tikvah where she gripped him about the waist.

Expression as cold as the tile under their feet, Sawaha seemed not the least sympathetic.

Before she could voice whatever accusation sat just inside her twisting lips, Tikvah blurted, "Please, Sawaha. Say nothing. He is gravely ill, and the night is bitter." Sawaha's glare did not relent, so Tikvah persisted, aiming her words at whatever crumb of a heart the laundress might possess. "Are we not all slaves? Does he not suffer enough already?"

Whether by Tikvah's plea or the moving of Yahweh Himself, a flash of something akin to pity flickered in the laundress's eyes. Her voice was as sharp as ever when she replied. "Where will you hide him?"

"Wine cellar." Tikvah panted under the strain of Shimshon's bulk. "Behind the empty amphorae."

Long, agonizing moments passed before Sawaha exhaled hard through her nose. She snatched a dark blanket from her pile and tossed it at Tikvah. "To hide under. Wait for my signal. I will clear the way."

Tikvah bundled the cover under her arm, knees trembling with relief. "For your mercy and aid, you have our thanks. May the Lord, the God of Israel, bless you."

Sawaha scoffed a laugh. "Thank your Babylonian lover. He threatened us with a throttling should we not assist if the need arose."

Lover? She could only mean Kala. Had he threatened the other slaves? When Tikvah opened her mouth, clarification on that point was not what emerged. "Kala is not my—"

"Whisht!" Sawaha pushed Tikvah, Shimshon with her, back around the corner, then stood before them while voices passed far too slowly in the adjoining corridor.

Beside her in the shadows, Shimshon's body jerked. A muted gag rang from him like a horn through the stillness.

Tikvah slapped a hand over the lower half of his face and prayed until Sawaha's urgent whisper cut through the tension.

"Now, *now*. And may your Jewish God protect you."

Releasing Shimshon's mouth, Tikvah gripped him fast by the arm and yanked him forward. Five steps more and she flung open the cellar door to breathe in the scents of musty earth and safety. "He already has," she said. "He already has."

Chapter 9

Though thou exalt thyself as the eagle, and though thou set thy nest among the stars, thence will I bring thee down, saith the Lord. (Obad. 4)

Tikvah, a deep voice whispered close to her ear.

Was it morning? Not yet. Sighing, she turned over.

A gentle hand shook her shoulder. **Up, Daughter.**

Sleep fogged her thoughts. *Abba?*

I am. Now, up. The hour is upon you.

The hour...the hour...

Gulping a breath, Tikvah shot to sitting. Her next blink obliterated the haze of slumber.

The hour!

Her head whipped to the wide-open window of the slave quarters. The rim of a moon hung less than a finger's width from the peak of its arc. Yahweh preserve her. She'd fallen asleep, and now the hour was—

The hour is upon us, the voice had said. Not a voice, but The Voice.

Indeed, that hour bore down on her with frightening speed.

You are good to me, Lord. Too good. For having closed her eyes even a moment, she deserved a lashing, if only of the tongue.

She hadn't intended to doze, much less fall into a stupor-inducing slumber. The plan had been to crawl under her thin blanket, same as always, and pretend sleep until snores filled the chamber. She would pass the time praying, then return to Shimshon and direct him to the heavy obstacles in the gate's path. Assuming, of course, he'd recovered enough to be in working condition.

When she'd left him, he'd been curled up in a tight ball, gripping his cramped stomach. Her only comfort—he'd finally kept liquid down. Before either of them had been ready, duty above had forced her to throw Sawaha's blanket over his shoulders and abandon him to a flask of water. She would have been missed, otherwise, and sparked questions best not asked.

The fact that Sawaha was aware of Shimshon's presence made her nervous enough. As evidenced by the quaking in her limbs.

Tikvah threw off the blanket covering her sandaled feet, gathered her twisted tunic, and launched upright. Just as the Hebrews on the first Passover, she'd gone to bed dressed and shod, prepared for flight.

And her *very own Moshe* was at *this very moment* outside the wall, trusting her to let him through. Him and his general and their uncounted soldiers with their gleaming swords, their ravish-hungry eyes, and their unlit torches. Which would burn soon enough.

She saw it all, and she had yet to step foot outside the slave chamber. Had not the tales of Babylon's capacity for death and destruction been handed down through the generations? Yerushalayim herself lay as testament to their lust for butchery.

Yahweh preserve me. Tikvah was about to unleash a beast. If she could get her shaking self through this maze of slumbering bodies without kicking someone awake. If she could navigate the house without detection. If she could aid Shimshon in moving those cumbersome amphorae. If she could roll back that stone before—

Something snagged the garment swishing at her ankle. Breath stuck in her throat. Tikvah froze mid-stride and looked down.

Unyielding fingers hooked about the hem of her tunic. Attached to them, the stiff arm of the last woman Tikvah would ever wish to encounter on such a dangerous venture as this.

Sawaha's dark eyes glittered impossibly bright in the chamber's obscurity. "What do you plot, girl?" Her whisper cut through the quiet like a cymbal clash.

Tikvah dropped into a crouch, grimacing at the loud pop of her knees, and slid a firm hand over Sawaha's mouth.

The woman did not flinch, did not blink. In fact, it felt as though her lips curled into a smile beneath Tikvah's palm.

Pulse galloping, Tikvah debated whether to lie.

She was going for fresh air. She was going to raid the pantry. She was going to visit the privy. All reasonable reasons for being up and about at this dark hour.

Would Yahweh disapprove? His *tisk* was almost audible in her heart. Where in a lie might trust be found? And if she could not trust Yahweh, whom could she?

The fingers about her hem relaxed and fell away.

Tikvah took it as confirmation. Truth it was. The help would be welcome, anyway. On less than a whisper, she said, "I am but a servant of Yahweh and of the great general, Belibni. Will you cry out, or will you join us in destroying our master?"

When Sawaha made no sound or motion either way, Tikvah ushered up a prayer and removed her hand, revealing the sly grin that had grown beneath it. She stayed her breath until Sawaha replied.

"Fetch my sandals, Jewess."

Despite the seriousness of the situation, Tikvah released an airy snort. "Fetch them yourself, Edomite." Then she extended a hand, palm up.

Sawaha engaged in a quiet, too-loud chuckle. She grasped Tikvah hard and nearly pulled her down as she used her weight as leverage to get herself up. The instant the woman was on her feet, Tikvah shook herself free and darted out the door.

Trusting Yahweh to go before her, Tikvah flew through the silent house and was out of breath by the time she reached the cellar door. On the top stair, she closed the door behind her, pausing only long enough to light the oil lamp stored in the niche to her left. Lamp nestled in her palm, she let her feet take the carved stone treads at speed, the *thud-thud-thud* of her footfalls sure to announce her presence.

But no. At the damp, musty bottom, the only thing to greet her was the rumble of profound slumber. Encouraging—her friend was not dead, not groaning in pain—but she would have to put an unfortunate end to his rest.

Bending at his side, she jostled his massive shoulder. "Abba, wake. Wake, hurry!" Not quite Yahweh's delicacy, but it served its purpose.

He bolted upright. "Eeh-ah?"

"Yes! The night has escaped me. Quickly now!" Twisting at the waist, she swung the light toward the rack of amphorae to assess the task ahead. "There is much we must—"

Her teeth clicked shut. The place did not look as she had left it.

Strewn about the space, four child-height, sealed amphorae lay on their sides. Their wooden rack, which was now empty, stood apart. In the space it once occupied, a cobweb-strung circular stone, red in hue, displayed itself in full view as if politely requesting to be rolled aside.

Her jaw loosed. She spun back to Shimshon. "You moved them! How?"

Grinning, he tapped his heart and jutted a finger toward the ceiling. "Ah-uh." He most certainly did not mean the master who slept above. But the Master who ruled and reigned and whose plan and purpose would not be hindered by a daughter who failed to keep her eyes open to pray.

Relief and gratitude washed over Tikvah in waves, pricking her eyes into a watery blur. "So He did, my friend." She blinked fast to unfog her vision, her sense of urgency somewhat abated, faith rolling in to replace it. "So He did."

"Well, Jewess, what is this plan of yours?" Sawaha spoke over Shimshon's shoulder. He made no move of surprise but tipped an ear in her direction.

Naturally, he'd already been alerted to her presence. Naturally, he'd listened to Yahweh, trusted His leading.

Tikvah gave his arm a reassuring pat. "Can you believe it, abba? Sawaha has joined our fight."

"Which is...? No, allow me a guess." Sawaha turned to the blocked entry and gave it a broad wave. "Your lover stands just the other side of that mule-sized stone."

"Presumably, yes," Tikvah replied, ignoring the reference to lovers. "Along with the might of the Babylonian army. Our task is to let them in."

Strolling to the stone, Sawaha rumbled a low, dark laugh. "I do like the sound of that. Most especially if that *might* leads to our pig of a master skewered on a spear and roasting in the fire of his own dwelling." She looked back to flash a wicked grin, the lamplight flickering eerily across her features, and Tikvah shuddered.

"What have they promised us?" Sawaha demanded.

Us? Tikvah joined the woman in assessing the stone from all directions, not bothering to correct this presumption either. If Sawaha bore into the task with diligence, Tikvah would fight for her liberation as well. "Freedom. Along with provisions and transport to Judah."

"Judah," Sawaha repeated. The word was not quite a sneer.

"You will not be obliged to travel our way." Tikvah did not have time for the woman's spite.

She ran her fingers over the seam where stone met the wall, knocking away accumulated dust. If the hole behind was as tall as the stone, a grown man would have only to duck his head to pass. The mass of it daunted.

Would even Shimshon, as strong and as practiced as he was, find himself overwhelmed? They would soon find out. He'd shuffled within a few strides of where they worked. She went to him and hooked onto his elbow.

"Debt to your god and to you will oblige me." *That* was a sneer, offered as only an embittered slave could.

Guiding Shimshon forward, Tikvah shook her head at Sawaha. "He would happily welcome your willing and devoted soul into His keeping. Here, abba. The stone to be rolled." Tikvah placed Shimshon's large hand against the stone's side. "That direction. May Yahweh Sabaoth give you strength."

"Omei." Nodding, he wedged his shoulder against the stone, braced his legs, and heaved.

It did not move. Did not emit so much as a creak of motion.

Sweat trickled along her spine as she beat back a surge of fear.

He adjusted his position and applied another grunting shove. Nothing. Only a squeak originating at its base on the opposite side.

Tikvah lowered the lamp to assess, while Sawaha squatted beside her, focus on Tikvah rather than the task at hand. "And you believe the general, that he will grant all he has promised?"

"I believe my God, the Lord of Hosts who goes before me." The Lord who split the sea. The same who would move this obstacle. *Please, Lord. A miracle.*

"Good enough for me."

It was? Tikvah's gaze wrenched up, but Sawaha no longer studied her.

Chin jutted, the woman squinted at the spot the stone stood. "Why do you crouch there gaping? Do you not see the mound of dirt? Dig it out!"

Tikvah looked to where Sawaha wagged a pointer finger. Indeed, a mound of packed earth had amassed in the track, serving as a wedge to prevent rolling. Tikvah loosed a triumphant "Ha!" and shoved the lamp at Sawaha. "Stay your efforts, Shimshon. I must clear the track."

She barely registered his murmur of acknowledgment over the pound of her heart and the rasp of her nails against the ground. Under her frenetic labor, they bent and cracked. Small sacrifice for great reward.

Within moments, she'd hacked through the impediment and scrambled back to her feet. "Try again, abba."

He retook his stance and threw himself into the labor. One heave. The stone groaned, then rolled with a terrible thunder. He stopped, breath sawing through his open mouth, every head turned to the stairs.

Short of Yahweh deafening the enemy above, there was little chance that racket had not carried throughout the structure.

"Tikvah!"

Her shoulders bounced. She spun toward the call of her name, spoken in a brusque whisper from behind her. From beyond Shimshon, too. It was then that she registered the cool air whirling through the cellar, bringing with it the fresh scent of night.

She hurried around Shimshon, skipping the leg he stretched behind himself as he once again bore into the stone. It rocked, giving way, and the fissure into the outside world expanded by a hand's width.

Wiggling fingers poked through the space. Large, calloused, masculine fingers attached to a warm voice. "Shalom, Tikvah."

She seized those fingers and squeezed, tears of joy and relief wetting her cheeks. "Shalom, Kala. Yes, yes, it is I! Shimshon too, and another woman who—"

A resounding squeal pierced the cellar's depths, the distinct sound of leather hinges complaining to an opening door.

Tikvah's body went rigid, but Sawaha lunged to blow out the lamp.

"Who is there?" a voice called from above.

Tikvah knew it by its nasal whine. Typically, it preceded the whine of the lash.

Aos, the author of her every scar.

None responded. For what would they say? *It is only us, Aos, two Hebrews and a traitorous laundress, arranging your imminent death.*

"Answer at once," he shouted down. "Or I raise the alarm!"

Sawaha sighed, loud and dramatic. "If you must know, it is myself, Aos."

A pause. "Who is myself?"

"Sawaha, fool."

"What business have you below at this hour? And what was the cause of that noise?" Light flooded the narrow staircase as Aos lit a torch. He took the first step down, holding out the torch before him, the tightness of his squinting eyes visible from where Tikvah stood two strides beyond the touch of light.

"Tikvah," Kala murmured through the crack. "Why have you stopped—"

"Whisht! Trouble," she whispered, catching his eyes through the gap. They shone large and dark, beautiful and too far from reach. Too far!

"There is a man with you?" Aos demanded, descending another step.

"What other business would I have in a musty cellar at this hour? Away with you. Leave us to our pleasure." Sawaha back-stepped, as if to block Shimshon from view, a fruitless attempt, for he neared twice her width, and he did not try to conceal himself. Rather, he propped against the stone, face lifted high, and lips moving with silent words.

"Eh? Perhaps I shall make it my business, as well." A lewd chuckle filtered through the chamber. Aos seemed to have forgotten the noise that brought him below, but if he took one more stair, the circle of his light would shed across them all, promptly reminding him.

Sawaha swore under her breath.

Tikvah gripped Shimshon's arm, ushering up a frantic, half-formed prayer. Sweat drenched her tunic, more so when she caught sight of the knife held at Aos's side.

He appeared to have forgotten it, too. The flames licked merrily in his glossy eyes as they scanned the space, taking in the layers he unpeeled.

Failure washed sour across Tikvah's tongue. She gulped it back as General Belibni's demand returned to her mind for a brutal reminder of all she'd promised him.

These things, he'd said, *in exchange for your unquestioning, unflinching service to Babylon in her quest for Edom's destruction.*

And what of her service to Yahweh? He had not placed her there, in that precise moment, to stand by and watch His word go unfulfilled. He had not placed that fragment of prophecy in her possession so she might hide it in the folds of her skirt and cower under the lash.

Tikvah's head turned. She met Kala's fear-widened gaze through the crack, apology written in her voice. "Forgive me, Kala."

His lashes flickered a blink. "Tikvah?"

"And thank you. For all you have, and would have, done." For choosing her, entrusting her with this mission, for offering her freedom, a home, and whatever future he'd shown her in those warm looks. Gifts. All of them.

"Thank— What? No, Tikvah," he stated, firmly, uselessly. "Tikvah, *stop*. Whatever you are thinking to do—"

She shut her ears to his pleas, for flickering orange light covered Shimshon's sightless face.

Did Aos see? No, he had eyes only for Sawaha who sashayed toward him, hips swaying, some honeyed invitation on her tongue. An effective, if unsettling, distraction.

Tikvah would not let it go to waste.

"Shimshon," she rasped into his ear. "Roll the stone. Roll it *now*." On that command, she rounded Sawaha. Feet light and swift, she rushed their enemy.

Aos's expression ranged from eyebrows shot high, to lips twisted in a welcoming leer, to mouth falling open at the ear-rattling grind of stone. His gaze darted behind her. "What is this!"

In the diversion, Tikvah hiked her tunic to her knees and threw herself at him. A leap, a crash. Their chests slammed together so hard he tipped backward. Arm flung back, he lost the torch somewhere behind him. It rolled, taking the bulk of the light with it.

He floundered, teetered. His alarm—half shock, half fury—hit her ear like a pig's squeal, sharp and high. Arms and legs wrapped tight about him, she rode out his fall.

The ground met her elbow with teeth-rattling force, wedging it under his torso. Her head bounced, and her chin nailed his collarbone. Blood filled her mouth, and a cry barreled up her throat. She caged it behind clamped teeth and tightened her grip against his violent thrash.

Every moment he stayed down, stayed occupied with *her*, was one less he could use to interfere with Shimshon. And one more Shimshon could use to get Kala through that entry.

Aos bucked again, roaring, cursing her God. The fool. Did he not consider the Source of her strength? Did he not know the full account of the Shimshon of old?

Fingernails ripped through her garment and into the skin of her back.

Tikvah registered the pain and locked her fingers harder around him.

"Hold on, girl!" Sawaha's shout buoyed Tikvah's resolve.

Aos aimed to undo it. He wrenched her by the hair, twisting her neck. Fire burned across her scalp.

It was pain. Nothing more. And she could give it back.

The instant he lightened his pull to switch tactics, she slammed her forehead into his face. Stars exploded across her vision. The metallic stench of blood crowded her nose.

His garbled blasphemy barely penetrated her awareness. The room spun too wildly. Her head drooped, but joints aching, she bore down. How much longer could she last?

He attempted a roll, but her left knee struck the ground, halting him. Curses and promises of death echoed through the chamber, but all she could hear was the sweet, unceasing grind of stone on stone.

Until blinding pain sliced into her side, and her own scream usurped all other sound. All other thought. Every muscle abandoned her, shrank away from the bloody knife raised high and glinting in the torchlight.

No...*the firelight.*

Aos's face, twisted by a murderous snarl, should not shine so brightly. No torch would blaze so fiercely.

It was then that Tikvah's ringing ears registered the crackle of fire, the heat growing at her back. Had his torch rolled into the wooden shelving? Panic fisted her heart.

But what did it matter if she burned? She would be dead already. Within moments. Her life sacrificed in obedience. Not a terrible way for a daughter of Zion to end her sojourn.

Arm raised, Aos paused. The tiniest of hesitations, the gathering of energy to strike. But in that breath, another struck first.

Out from the darkness came the swing of a jar. It connected with the man's temple and exploded in a shower of liquid and shards of clay. Olives thudded about her, then the knife. It landed blade down in the dirt at her hip, distracting from the slow crash of Aos's limp body. Eyes rolled high in his head, he tipped sideways and fell face-first in a puddle of sour-smelling vinegar water.

Tikvah wriggled away, positioning her feet to kick him in the nose should he move. She stared, gaze pinning him where he lay. Mouth open, she panted through shock and pain and dared the man to wake.

"Stupid girl!" Sawaha was suddenly before her, blocking her view of all but the woman's skirt. "Stupid, stupid girl. Throwing yourself at him that way! Have you killed yourself?" She scrabbled at Tikvah's garment, tugging, yanking.

Tikvah let loose a groan. She clutched her side, curling over it. Sticky warmth oozed through the cracks of her fingers.

Muttering obscenities, Sawaha pressed hard into the wound and wrenched a scream from deep in Tikvah's chest.

Time and thought blurred. Nothing mattered. Not the roaring fire or the silent stone. Not the unconscious guard or the fuming laundress. In that moment, Tikvah managed no more than to move air through her lungs.

Shimshon pushed Sawaha aside. His mouth opened for a long, stricken cry, and his large hands fumbled about her, patting her knee, her shoulder, her head. He pulled her close against his body, his heat sinking into her cooling skin.

Tikvah would comfort him, but her working jaw would not produce sound.

Pounding footfalls broke through her haze, as did a bark of alarm. "What did you do!"

Kala? He did not sound the same.

Eyelids heavy as lead, Tikvah could not see to learn. And her hearing buzzed, the vibration of an armed legion charging past.

She exhaled.

Muffled voices shouted, one of them female.

"You cannot help her! Back away, man." Yes, that was Kala, using his harsh soldier's voice. "Give her to me."

Shimshon leaned over and dropped a kiss onto her forehead, then pulled away and extended his arms, Tikvah in them. Space opened beneath her, a heartbeat only, before another swooped in to bracket her with his arms.

Agony ripped through her center.

"Save...Sawaha," she slurred.

Then, the aroma of spice engulfed her, along with an all-consuming dark.

Chapter 10

Shall I not in that day, saith the Lord, even destroy the wise men out of Edom, and understanding out of the mount of Esau? And thy mighty men, O Teman, shall be dismayed, to the end that every one of the mount of Esau may be cut off by slaughter. For thy violence against thy brother Jacob shame shall cover thee, and thou shalt be cut off for ever. (Obad. 8–10)

Edom burned.

Or so Tikvah had been told five days after the fact when she'd opened her eyes to her first morning not dominated by pain, fever, and irresistible slumber. That was yesterday.

Try as she might, Tikvah did not recall being carried down the mountain and housed in the women's tent.

Pitched at the protected center of the Babylonian army camp, it housed the wives of a few mid-ranking officers and the Hebrew women affiliated with Kala and his fellow liaisons, including his mother and sister. Tikvah and Sawaha rounded out their numbers to ten.

Eleven, if one included Shimshon. From the start, he'd stationed himself at Tikvah's sickbed and refused to budge during the daylight hours. His sightless eyes and helping hands earned him both pity and favor of the women. So, there he stayed, willing to leave only once the women filed back in for the night.

Over the last day, several had come and gone. Presently, they were out, engaged in the various chores that earned their keep in a man's army. With only Shimshon for company, Tikvah lay unmoving on a stack of cushions, shallow breaths lifting the linen sheet that thwarted the evening chill. When she did not stir, the pain was bearable. But then, any pain was better than the death that had stormed through Busayra.

"Absolute destruction," Captain Namtar had informed her earlier while taking a report for the general. His eyes still shone with the blaze of battle when he added, "Not one stone left atop another."

Precisely as prophesied.

General Belibni had been happy to fulfill the prophecy to the letter. His soldiers had slaughtered and plundered. They stripped the land of its fruit and its people of their

pride. In short, Edom was brought low, as Yahweh foretold.

Death. So much death.

"Do not trouble yourself over that now." Those words
had come from Tikvah's gentle nurse, Adva, who, as it
turned out, was Kala's sister.

Upon learning of their relation, Tikvah's cheeks red-
dened. The fever to blame. Or so she'd said.

"They have got our old master naked, chained, and
waiting." Sawaha clucked her disdain when she'd arrived
to gossip—and to ensure Tikvah's word on her reward.
"For what, I cannot guess. Your recovery perhaps. What
a shame it would be for the worm's betrayer to miss his
execution."

At that, whatever blood had rushed to Tikvah's cheeks
on reflection of Kala drained straight away. She had no
desire to watch a man suffer. Not even the odious Master
Zerah. When she'd muttered as much, Sawaha spat half a
curse, halted by a sharp look from Adva, then swallowed
as if downing a bitter herb. She'd stomped from the army
tent on grumbling instructions for Tikvah to rest and heal.

"You are a good woman and the daughter that I love."
Though silent, Shimshon spoke those words through the
squeeze of her hand, his perpetual presence, and his new
stylus and wax tablet. Since sundown of the previous day,
the time of her waking, the stylus had not ceased its careful
movements over the wax. Every little while, there came a

tap on her arm and a tablet thrust under her nose—nigh on ten years of dammed-up speech bursting forth.

A question after her comfort. A word of love. A reflection on God's goodness.

Weary as she was, she cherished every small communication. She, too, felt the loss of his voice, mourned never hearing it again. She yearned to know what deep thoughts ran through that wise head of his, to understand the man Yahweh considered His servant.

Thank the Lord for His abundant mercy, they now had time for it. Years more if Kala had his way.

He came by once, briefly, that she was aware of—within the hour of the first flutter of her lashes. She remembered the visit little better than she did the trek down the mountain. Sawaha later filled her in. The few moments they'd shared included tears on her part, stoic relief on his.

Also according to Sawaha, after Tikvah blacked out in the cellar, Kala risked his general's wrath by putting aside his sword to see her placed into proper care. Although, from the way she relayed the tale, the sword hadn't been set aside so much as repurposed in threats against the first healer they'd found. Rather, the first who'd not already been run through by Babylonian iron.

Whoever he was, the man could thank Tikvah's wound and Kala's determination for the fact that he yet lived. The rest of his family, per the telling, had perished, as had most in Busayra. A few remained, children and maidens. All taken into captivity.

Tikvah understood their plight all too well. Understood, commiserated, bore the weight of their misery. If not for her, those innocents would be safe in their homes. At the outset of her mission, she'd been so firm in her support of God's justice that the notion of the resulting bloodshed hardly registered.

The reality of it, however—the death and suffering of others—was a harder portion to swallow than she'd expected. Not that she'd thought on it much, focused as she'd been on not getting her own self killed. But now...

Guilt climbed her spine. She shivered, and it had nothing to do with the evening breeze ushering in the clangor and rank odors of an army camp. Soul heavy, she let her head fall to the side against her pillow.

Shimshon, the reminder of her purpose, snoozed on the ground to her right. Otherwise, he would be doting on her like a vigilant grandmother, patting her forehead for fever, checking her toes for a chill, as he'd done since she woke from her fever. Blind he may be, but he exhibited a special sense for her discomfort.

Nothing escaped him, not so much as a shiver. Unless he was snoring.

A soft smile curved her lips as she gazed at him, grateful beyond measure for this second abba she'd been given. When she returned to Judah, would she find her first?

Would she recognize him if she did? Her memory had long since lost the image of the man. Imma's face, however, that lovely twist-toothed smile and crinkle-eyed tease, had emblazoned itself into Tikvah's mind.

Soon, Imma. Soon, I will return to you. And what a story of God's goodness she would tell. The prospect multiplied the joy budding within her, blossoming it across her mouth.

"Never was there a sight more beautiful than Tikvah bat Aharon awake and smiling."

Shimshon stirred, and Tikvah's head snapped toward the tent's entry and the soldier occupying its center.

Kala. Her heart wobbled, silly thing.

Earlier, Adva had tied the entry flap back to let in the cooler evening breezes. Now, soft pink light outlined Kala's broad form and cast his features in shadow. But no light was required to appreciate the picture he cut. Even that odious Babylonian helmet and could not detract from the vision of manly strength standing before her. The uniform might even—as much as it pained her to think it—have added to it.

Few other Hebrews could claim to have garnered mighty Babylon's attention and respect, or to have been used in such a role to accomplish Yahweh's purpose. Daniel came to mind, that exile-turned-prophet who'd become an adviser to King Nebuchadnezzar. There were others, too, who excelled in faith during these recent trials, names written in scrolls to be passed along from priest to congregation, father to son.

Would any recall Kala's daring, his resourcefulness and audacious yet faith-filled arrangement with Judah's overlord? Doubtful any would record his name in sacred scrolls, but Yahweh saw, and Tikvah would remember as would her children.

Possibly...*their* children? With the way Kala looked at her just then—body held tight and expectant, leaning toward her as if compelled or scarcely restrained—she could almost believe he was imagining it too. Their future. Or, perhaps, that he was moments from waking Shimshon to request a marriage contract.

There went her absurd heart again, jumping up and down in her chest like a puppy in sight of a juicy morsel of lamb. Could Kala hear it across the way? Could he see the blush staining her neck? The tent's dim light might disguise her growing infatuation. Distractions worked as well.

She *tsk*ed at him, all feigned disapproval. "How bold that uniform makes you."

His chuckle was all rumbling masculinity. "My admiration emboldens me."

As if to prove his claim of boldness, he removed his helmet and entered on a soldier's crisp stride. He stopped at the foot of her bed of cushions, giving her a clear view of the admiration he claimed. It beamed from the eyes he settled on her.

But she did not deserve it. "Turn your gaze upward," she murmured, turning her own downward to the hands twisting her lap. "For I would be nothing without our Lord." She did not deserve his esteem. She did not deserve the plate of honeyed dates beside her or the cushions beneath her. None should praise any part of war or destruction, even if those who'd engaged in it followed Yahweh's lead.

Kala replicated her clucking noise. "If you wish to deflect my esteem, praising Yahweh is not the way of it."

"What *is* the way of it? Taking up the gods of the land?" Not that she would, but she was curious to know what might drive Kala away. Did he comprehend what she'd done? Had he pieced it together?

Shimshon grunted beside her, having sat up scowling. She snagged his hand and held onto it as she might a tether holding her above Busayra's steepest cliff.

Kala crossed his arms in a relaxed pose. "That would indeed repel me, or..." His gaze traveled beyond her shoulder and went vacant a bare moment before coming back to her honed with something resembling affection. "No, there is nothing else."

She spluttered a laugh. "Nothing at all? Are you certain? What if I had a penchant for smelly cheese?"

Shaking his head in disapproval, Shimshon withdrew his hand from her sweaty grasp and began beating his flattened pillow into better shape.

"Malodorous cheese?" Kala asked. "That is the worst of you?"

"What if I convulsively howl at the moon?"

"I might be convinced to howl with you." His grin became impish.

Though tempted to continue with him down this lighter path, she must not. The smile dissolved off her. "What if I'd...killed a man?"

"Whom do you mean?" When her eyes fill with tears, he demolished the space between them and lowered to a knee, taking her fingers between his own. "For what he did to you, I took that Edomite's life. Me." He thumped his chest. "I did. My sword. You did not kill that man."

Oh, she most certainly had. At the mental assertion, her muscles tensed and pain charged through her abdomen. She hissed an inhale and settled a hand over the spot. "No...I have killed *many*."

"Tikvah, enough. You pain yourself." He smoothed a palm over her forehead, but the tightness there remained.

Eyes shutting tight, she wagged her head. "By letting in the Babylonian army, I am responsible for the deaths of—" Her throat closed off, but Kala would not have let her continue, regardless.

Calloused fingers pressed against her mouth. "Shah, Tikvah. Not so."

She blinked wet lashes at him, unable to halt the tears cascading over his fingertips. Gentle and patient, he brushed them away. As quickly as they fell, he did away with them. "When Moshe crossed the sea," he said, voice a scratchy bass, "was it his sword that slew the Egyptian army foolish enough to follow?"

Throat thick with tears, she could only sniff and give her head a small shake.

"Correct. And when Joshua blew the trumpets outside Jericho, whose strength was it that tumbled the walls?"

To that, Tikvah said nothing. Words were unnecessary here. Kala knew she followed his meaning. Slave in a foreign land she might be, but no part of her childhood lessons in the Torah had gone to the wayside. In their short time together, he'd surely come to understand that much about her. From his satisfied grunt, she deemed her assumption correct.

And she deemed herself corrected. Though tempted to continue in self-reproach, doing so gave herself the credit and detracted from Yahweh's will and might.

Kala pulled back a bit to straighten her rumpled cover. As if he might with the same ease straighten her tangled reasoning, he carried on. "As sure as if an army of angels entered that cellar, the Lord of Hosts slew the Edomites.

And did He not warn them? Did He not send His prophet with a message?"

At mention of that message, Tikvah's gaze flicked to Shimshon's place but found it vacated. At what point did he leave? "Shimshon can be sneaky when he wishes to be." Tikvah chuffed a watery laugh.

Brow furrowing, Kala cocked his head at her, then looked to the spot Shimshon had once occupied. For long moments, he studied the empty, dented cushion. "Is Shimshon his true name?"

Tikvah sniffed, unable to contain her smile, for she'd seen that question forming in his mind. "It is the name given to him the day my master learned of our judge from history, Shimshon, and the ways his enemy, the Philistines, tortured him. He'd gleaned it off an itinerant trader in copper. Not to be outdone by the Philistines in cruelty, he renamed our friend, put out his eyes, and sent him to the miller with orders to tie him to the millstone."

Tikvah did not witnessed it, Yahweh be praised. Just the same, her stomach churned anew at the memory of Shimshon's bloodied face and trembling body as he'd fought the shock.

The color leached from Kala's cheeks. He lowered his head and engaged in a short time of respectful silence. At last, his throat lurched with a swallow. "That mockery of a name, Shimshon, should have burned with Edom.

What name did his abba give him?" Kala's eyes tightened in serious contemplation. "Is it perhaps...Obadyah?"

Tikvah only smiled.

When Kala realized she would not answer, he quirked his lips. "Very well. I shall ask *him*." He withdrew the little scrap of parchment, the words of the Lord as spoken to the prophet. "I believe this is yours."

Reverence filtered through her. She took the wrinkled parchment and held it in the fist she laid over her heart. "Not mine. I simply guarded it." As was requested of her.

"And you did it well." His timbre dropped, that admiration once more warming his eyes. "So well."

No hiding it this time. Her cheeks flamed. In reaction to his praise? To the attraction he did not bother to hide? For yes, this close, no able-minded woman could miss it.

Nose a bit too prominent, front tooth as twisted as her mother's, Tikvah was no great beauty, which was how she knew to trust Kala's attraction. He looked inward to the place her soul resided, where it leaned toward him, speaking his language.

Even so, she felt ill-prepared to address such weighty matters. They remained in a Babylonian army camp under the fickle eye of King Nabonidus, and would until her wound healed enough to allow travel.

General Belibni might have promised them his protection, but Tikvah would not breathe fully again until they put many days' travel between them and the King of the Four Corners of the World.

Then there was the matter of cleaning up the last of the filth. She swallowed convulsively. "Kala, I've no wish to see Master Zerah's death." The thought set her hands to twisting at the blanket.

Kala took them securely between his own, a crease digging into the space between his brows. "At dawn, Zerah stood before the king and answered for his crimes. He is dead, and you have no master, save the Lord."

Master Zerah. Dead.

Relief slumped her. Or was it grief?

Whichever the case, a weight suddenly converged on her from all sides, pressing her into the cushions and drooping her eyes. "I am so weary."

A smile, part-sad, part-doting, crested Kala's lips. With tender care, he tucked her arms under the cover. "Then rest, Tikvah of my heart. Until you can stand again, I will stay near."

The blessed sound of that finished closing her eyes. "And after?"

"After…"

He took so long to respond that she cracked her eyelids to see if he'd left. Instead, she found him gazing on her with the unspoken promises of a man who'd decided on a matter. A now-familiar look, it said, *After, we will be one.*

When he opened his smiling mouth, however, all he said was, "Judah."

Chapter 11

But upon mount Zion shall be deliverance,
and there shall be holiness; and the house of
Jacob shall possess their possessions. (Obad. 17)

T he scurry of Tikvah's feet lifted clouds of dust that
clung to the hem of her tunic, staining the coarse
linen a reddish brown. Eyes on the path before her, she
imagined Sawaha's strident rebuke. Something, no doubt,
about staying in the grassy patches instead of walking the
trails worn bare and dusty by the soldiers' tramping feet.
Something else about the time it would take to scrub it
clean, the loss of skin on her knuckles, the ache in her back.

The woman was a boundless font of criticism, but Tikvah was coming to learn that she contrived most of it, for
at the woman's center lay a wounded heart longing for
love. Happy to provide such, Tikvah delighted in Sawaha's
shocked responses to overtures of affection.

She would have smiled at the memory of Sawaha's most recent fluster at Tikvah's compliments on her work, if not for the fingers pinching Tikvah's upper arm, dragging her along against her will. The conical desert tent looming large before her also played a part in her sober bearing.

The red squares of the fabric's decorative design faded under the same rich hues cast by the sun setting at her back. Sabbath was upon them; although, not a soul in the camp, apart from Tikvah and the half-dozen affiliated with Kala, cared one whit. Certainly not the general who'd summoned Tikvah from her couch.

"The girl should not be moved!" Adva had protested to the soldier who'd burst into their tent a moment ago, spouting commands. "Is it a split wound you want on her, eh? After all my care!"

"Out of my way, woman. I have orders to follow." On that merciless note, he'd hauled Tikvah to her feet and out into the evening, grumbling as he went along. "What difference would one night make, anyway?"

The soldier referred to the remainder of her convalescence. At dawn, the camp would pluck up their stakes, roll their tents, and march on.

Because they'd enjoyed success overtaking Edom, General Belibni deemed Kala's contract complete. While his army pushed toward Tayma in Arabia, Kala and his retinue—including Tikvah, Shimshon, and Sawaha—would depart for Judah.

These uplifting thoughts accompanied Tikvah into General Belibni's tent and onto her knees before him. Pain knifed into her side as she battled the fear lurking at the corners of her mind. What might the general of Babylon's army want with her at this late hour of their acquaintance? Nothing good, she suspected.

His low-voiced greeting confirmed it. "You deceived me, little Tikvah Jewess."

The man reclined before a spread of bowls, modest in quantity for a general of his repute. He dragged a piece of flat bread across the bottom of a dish while watching her from under hooded eyes.

Several men surrounded him. Aside from the unobtrusive guards at his back, a man sat cross-legged some strides away, a lap desk balanced on his knees. The wax tablet on the surface, along with the various parchments stacked about him, named him a scribe.

In addition to those attendants, Captain Namtar dined beside the general, managing a smug smile despite his fat cheek and vigorous chewing. Why should *he* be so pleased with himself?

It took Tikvah those moments of observation for the general's accusation to register. *Deception?* Her throat lurched, and her mind whirred. "My lord?"

General Belibni placed the bread in his mouth, then flicked a commanding finger.

One guard launched into motion. He slipped into the deep shadows of the tent's far edges and emerged with Shimshon in tow.

Air ripped through her nose, a sharp inhale that choked off at the agony spearing her middle. She gripped the wound and pushed off the ground. Teetering and dizzy, she leaned over the hand flattened to her side and panted through the pain. Her mouth opened to spout demands for an explanation, but caution bid her snap it shut again. Until she understood what this was about, she must not risk the general's vexation.

The sight of Shimshon's ravaged face stoked a fierce possessiveness in her. If the general dared harm him, the meager control she maintained over her tongue and anger would not hold.

Shimshon stumbled forward, his feet catching on the edge of a thick rug. The guard's clasp on his arm prevented a fall, but not the humiliation. Head bowed, Shimshon righted himself as best his bent posture allowed and shuffled on. They halted at the far side of the plush carpet stretching beneath Tikvah's feet.

The guard released him and backed away.

Shimshon remained standing, his entire body angled toward the sounds of her ragged breaths.

"Do not worry yourself over me, abba. I am out of breath from the walk, only that."

He frowned his doubt, a deep scoring of weathered skin.

Before she could continue reassurances, the general spoke. "Mm, yes, I see the father tendencies. But where is the shepherd you claimed will guard and guide you on your journey to Judah? This man can do neither."

Tikvah narrowed her eyes, understanding settling in like a malaise. So this was about their barter.

Why quibble now, though? Shimshon had been at her side since Babylon breached Busayra's walls. And according to Adva, the day after the battle, Kala had brought him and Sawaha before Captain Namtar for official permission to lodge in the camp. None had hidden Shimshon's blindness or whitewashed his limitations.

Had the captain not relayed his misgivings until now? For what purpose?

Or was this about the general's desires? Perhaps he would use Shimshon as a weapon of manipulation. In either case, only a show of strength would see her through this without loss.

Tikvah faced the general and drew her shoulder blades together to avoid appearing weak. "I never said guard and guide. Only that he was familiar with the wilderness, and he would be with me."

Captain Namtar chortled and pointed to Tikvah. "Did I not tell you her tongue had two edges, General? That you should proceed with caution?"

General Belibni cast his gaze to the tent's peak. "Yes, thank you, Captain. Without your wisdom, I would be wandering circles in the desert." He shoved the nearest dish away from himself and sat straighter, his dark eyes descending to Tikvah. "Regardless of your wording, what you implied was—"

Raised voices beyond the tent preceded a soldier bursting in, ducking through the low opening. Latched to his arm and protesting vociferously, another fellow followed him through. The intruder stopped short just inside and came erect.

"Kala!" His name blew out of Tikvah's mouth and wrenched his eyes in her direction.

Air exploded from his chest in a gust. He shucked off the guard's clasp, ignoring the man's profuse apologies to the general, and took a forward step.

General Belibni lifted a halting palm, silencing the guard and freezing Kala mid-step. "Soldier, I expect you will have a good reason for losing your sanity and invading my presence."

As though he'd sprinted to arrive, Kala's chest rose and fell in great heaves. Through them, he rectified his stance, bending at the waist, and extended a cupped palm. He lowered it before him in acknowledgment of his lesser status. "May there be well-being to my lord, the general."

General Belibni rolled his hand in an impatient gesture, urging Kala on.

"When I learned you summoned Tikvah, I came at once to be of help. For I am your faithful liaison, the voice between yourself and all peoples of the region."

Captain Namtar huffed a dry laugh. "Well done, Jew."

The general's lips screwed up. "Interesting you did not force your presence upon us while I interviewed Sawela, that prickly Edomite slave woman."

"*Sawaha*, my lord." Kala spoke from his bowed position. "And Tikvah is my people. As such, she is of greater concern to me."

Sighing dramatically, the general swung his head in Namtar's direction. "Are all young men in love such fools?"

"Why look at *me* for the answer to that question?"

Why ask it at all? Tikvah stared at General Belibni as though to drill through his skull for his purpose in the meeting. What did he *want*?

"Well, certainly not because you are young," the general replied.

Perplexity stole over Captain Namtar's features, and Tikvah wondered what skills recommended the captain to General Belibni's service.

"Fools," the general went on, "and wholly predictable."

Brows drawing in, Kala opened his mouth as if to speak.

The general cut him off. "Save it for after I have concluded with the woman. Take this down." He wagged a hand at the scribe, who bent over the tablet at once, stylus poised.

General Belibni returned his attention to Tikvah. "Under the authority given me by rights of war and privilege, I hereto transfer your slavery and that of your two friends to my household. The Edomite professed experience in the laundry, which she will resume in slavery to me. As for where I shall employ you...what labor did you do for Zerah?"

"My lord!" Kala dared another step forward.

Head whipping Kala's direction, the general showed him and the tent that very authority, his scowl of fury hot enough to singe the air Tikvah sucked into her lungs. He waited until Kala, though snorting air like a bull, lowered his head and relaxed his posture, before sliding his gaze back to Tikvah. "Well?"

"S-slavery?" Heart pounding madly in her throat, Tikvah glanced about the space.

Hands folded loosely before him, Shimshon stood at ease, not a hint of perturbation about him. Had he not heard the general? Or had she misunderstood?

Her eyes darted next to Kala, whose expression validated her own shock and confusion. The muscle of his jaw bulged, and he had yet to recover his breath. Returning her steady gaze, he shook his head, two tiny jerking motions that said *I did not know* and *I will not cede.*

He would fight for her. And he would lose. His position, his substance, his life.

The malaise in her gut cycloned itself into full-on nausea. For Kala and whatever foolishness would end him. For her own loss of hope. For Sawaha and Shimshon.

Shimshon.

He remained as he'd been, as calm as if the Lord God were even then whispering messages of reassurance and peace into his ear. He likely was.

Tikvah's heart backed down from her throat. If Shimshon could stand firm in his faith and in Yahweh's purpose for them both, so could she.

Had He not delivered them from the Egyptians and from the Edomites? Had He not also sworn on His holiness to deliver them from Babylon?

She returned her focus to the general and willed steadiness into her voice. "You violate our agreement."

"Do you refer to the agreement I made on grounds of deception?" He pointed a stiff finger at Shimshon. "Your shepherd cannot protect you or provide for you, and I cannot very well release you to your own care. Then there is the issue of your deliberate trickery, which cannot go unpunished."

"Punished! It is not my fault you failed to ascertain the details before accepting the barter."

"Careful, little Tikvah Jewess," General Belibni rumbled low and menacing, eyes tightening on her. "You tread where strong men of war venture not."

"And *you*," she said, voice rising with ire, "a distinguished general of the great King Nabonidus, break your vow to me."

"Bah." He swatted the air before his nose as he might with a noxious odor. "I swore to free you of Duke Zerah and of Edom. The first is accomplished. The second will be at dawn when we draw up stakes and move north. I see no broken vow." Here, he leisurely shifted attention to Kala. "Do you, *liaison*?"

As a straining coil at last sprung free, Kala propelled himself toward the general, stripping off the gold bands adorning his forearms as he went. He tossed them at the general's feet. While they rolled to a stop, he dropped to a knee, head bent in deference. "Did you not admire these, my lord? Have them. Only give me the woman and her companions in return."

"Why, yes," General Belibni replied, tone gracious. "I believe I will."

"What?" Tikvah blurted.

Kala's head popped up. "Y-you will?"

"I've neither the desire nor the need of additional slaves, but I cannot let the women go without an able benefactor. In exchange for the three slaves, I accept your two golden cuffs."

Relief poured through Tikvah like desert rain, flagging her knees. She locked them before they could give out. Had it really been that simple? No, it had not. Regret pursued her relief. It had been costly, as well. How much had Kala relied on that gold for re-establishment in Judah?

"You have my abundant gratitude, General Belibni." Kala's head dipped again, lower than before. "May Yahweh grant long life to you, to your kin, and to your herds."

"Indeed, I covet the blessing of such a god," General Belibni replied, more humbly than Tikvah had yet heard him.

Of no such spiritual persuasion, Captain Namtar stretched to reach the bowl nearest the general. "You might have gone about the matter a simpler way, General."

For once, Tikvah and the captain agreed. General Belibni had the power to do whatever he wished—as the evening proved. Why toy with them?

"Ah, but look," the general said. "This way, I rid myself of their hungry mouths while forcing the hand of the young and foolish. The boy might have taken until the harvest month to gather the courage to voice his affection."

"Has he voiced affection? I did not hear."

"And look, I've gained two beautiful cuffs for my wife." He gestured to the glittering adornment with a jerk of his head. "Retrieve them."

Grumbling, Captain Namtar rose to his knees and crawled the two steps to collect the bands. He sat back on his thighs and buffed one against his chest. "Why not simply take them from the man?"

"I prefer gold to be thrown at my feet." General Belibni bared every tooth in a grin that was more disturbing than amusing.

To which Captain Namtar blew his lips like a horse. "You prefer dramatics. Otherwise, you would have chosen the siege over"—he brandished a jeweled hand to take in Kala and Tikvah—"them."

General Belibni stroked his oiled beard. "Quite true."

"As is most of what I say."

A frown dragged at the general's mouth. "Are there no river beasts for you to squeal at, you braying ass?"

Tikvah couldn't help it. She laughed, a single blurt of humor that morphed in a groan of pain.

General Belibni gave the captain a long baleful look that ended with a sudden snap of the fingers toward Kala. "You. Can you not see your woman is in agony? Return her to her rest. My scribe will draw up the record of sale and have it delivered."

"Yes, my lord. Thank you, my lord." Kala was on his feet in a moment, bowing his way backward. He reached for Tikvah and scooped her off her feet.

Her wound pulled, and a whimper escaped her.

"I know, I know," Kala soothed. "Bear up. I will have you reclining before long."

The scent of spice, which was all Kala, engulfed her in a comforting wave. Hooking her arms about his neck, she released herself to his care.

Adjusting her gently in his hold, he crossed to Shimshon and bumped him with his elbow. "My arm, Shimshon."

"Eeh-ah?" Shimshon inquired as they set out. Despite Kala's brisk stride, Shimshon patted about until he found her head and stroked loose hair from her forehead.

"Have no concern for me, abba," she said through gritted teeth. "No damage done." Except perhaps to her heart. The thing had yet to find its rhythm.

As Kala ducked through the tent opening, he used the opportunity to murmur in her ear. "Tikvah, forgive me. I should have thought to—"

"Voiced your affection, then wedded me at first opportunity?"

Shimshon chuckled.

An adorable blush stole over Kala. "Yes. Quite true."

Though the sweat of pain broke out on her forehead, she reached for the joy brought on by freedom from the general's tent and released it in a tease. "As is most of what I say."

"Oi! Listen to the woman, Shimshon. She quotes a pagan."

"Yahweh speaks through asses, too. Best you remember that."

Shimshon huffed a laugh, drawing a pout from Kala.

He said, "I see now how things will be, the two of you rallied against me."

"Did you not say you are a better man when subjected to a woman's blunt tongue?" In emphasis, Tikvah poked his chest, pleased beyond the grin stretching her cheeks. For Kala had owned her heart long before he tossed gold at the general's feet.

Beneath her, his torso rocked with a laugh. "In that case, how else might you rebuke me? Please, make me a better man."

"I shall leave it at that for now. But if you do not wed me upon arrival in Judah, you will feel the sharpest edge of my tongue."

"Upon arrival? Not before?"

Was that disappointment weighing his tone? A careful peering into his eyes revealed only that penetrating look, the one that spoke of future secrets known only to them two, and to Yahweh above who'd ordained them.

At the intimacy suggested in his eyes, her pulse danced, but she did not avert her gaze. Let him understand she would not shy from him or his secrets. Let him see that she embraced them. Or would once they'd exchanged vows before God.

On that reminder of propriety, she considered her message sent and averted her eyes to the breathtaking reds streaking the western sky.

"Do you know what the Lord said to the prophet Jeremiah regarding the brides of Yerushalayim?"

The question piqued her interest. "Tell me."

"Again there shall be heard in Yerushalayim," Kala began in the solemn tone of recitation, "the voice of joy and the voice of gladness, the voice of the bridegroom and the voice of the bride, the voice of those who will sing: *Praise the Lord of hosts, for the Lord is good, for His mercy endures forever.* For I will cause the captives of the land to return as at the first."

Her heart leaped. "Does the passage mean us?"

Kala said nothing for a long while, only trod smoothly through the quieting camp. She barely jostled in his muscular arms, his care of her clear in every deliberate placement of his tread—an apt picture of how tenderly Yahweh cared for His children.

As every good and loving Father, He disciplined for correction. But His mercies were abundant and His faithfulness sure through every generation. His promises did not fail.

"I do not think so, Tikvah of my heart." Though Kala's words did not contain the happiest answer, he did not utter them in sadness, but in contemplative faith. "Daniel prophesied seventy years from the beginning of Exile until the return. We are not yet halfway through. Yerushalayim today is no doubt inhospitable to us. Neither has the Lord authorized our return to rebuild the walls or the Temple.

Our destination lies in the Galil and the vineyards we will work for our fathers and for Babylon's treasury.

"But our children..." A slow grin transformed his handsome features into a view no young woman should be subjected to without the right to close the door on a shared chamber.

Heat scorched her cheeks. "Our...children? What of them?"

"They will sing, Tikvah. In the streets of Yerushalayim, they will sing." Kala stopped between a row of tents and, as if one, they looked toward the northwest horizon where the Holy City lay under the deepening purple of encroaching night.

Even Shimshon turned his face north. Might he sense God's presence there?

As far as Tikvah was concerned, His presence could not be stronger than the peace enveloping them there in Babylon's camp.

Our children...

Yes, their children, and *their* children, and the children of generations she could not fathom, would praise the Lord of Hosts in the City of David.

For He is good.

Indeed, He would be good to them in Judah, as He had been good to her there. Uplifting her, sustaining her, providing companionship and even a husband.

For Yahweh was not confined to stone or to wood or to any other brazen image seated mute in a shrine. No ark or temple or even a city could confine Him. The Creator could be found the world over, even in a Babylonian camp in the Kingdom of Edom.

Lifting her face to the heavens, she let fly the worship rising to her lips. "My hope does not lie in man or in a city, oh Lord, but in you. Only in you is it fulfilled. For you are everlastingly good, and your mercy endures forever."

Close at her side, Shimshon finished the prayer with a solemn, "Omei."

"Omein." Kala tightened his embrace and placed gentle lips at Tikvah's temple.

Together, they smiled and returned their sight to the evening star shining with promise over the horizon.

Thanks for reading!

Two things before you go.

1. Go deeper into Edom and its fall in *Knowing Obadiah*, a Christian women's Bible commentary.

2. When you subscribe to my monthly newsletter, you get two free Christian ebooks.

Turn the page to learn more.

VISIT THE AUTHOR'S WEBSITE FOR E-GIFTS:
www.aprilgardner.com/fireandflame-freebies

1. **Beautiful in His Sight**, a Christian WWI Romance set during the Halifax Explosion. (e-book). *Jack is her freedom. Silas, her salvation. God? He's the building that buries her.*

2. **The Red Feather**, Christian Native American Historical (ebook and digitally narrated audio). *Amidst the clash of weapons, two lives intertwine in a battle for love, faith, and survival.* Experience a vivid frontier setting and an enemies-to-lovers story that will render you breathless.

What to Read Next

- *A Hope Fulfilled*, a novella of biblical Edom and Obadiah's prophecy
- *Knowing Obadiah*, a Christian Women's Bible Commentary
- *But in Mount Zion*, a companion study (personal or small group) for *Knowing Obadiah*

Can be read in any order.
Learn more and purchase at www.aprilgardner.com.

About the Author

APRIL W GARDNER is an editor and award-winning author of Christian fiction. Enjoy April's other books:

HISTORICAL ROMANCE

Beneath the Blueberry Moon Series (Native American)

Drawn by the Frost Moon Series (Native American)

Beautiful in His Sight (WW1, standalone)

Better than Fiction (WW1 era, dual-timeline)

BIBLICAL STUDY/FICTION

A Fire and a Flame Series

CHILDREN'S MIDDLE GRADE HISTORICAL

Lizzie and the Guernsey Gang (WW2 standalone)

WRITING CRAFT

Body Beats to Build On

CONTACT:

Facebook: April.Gardner1

Website: AprilGardner.com

Email: info@aprilgardner.com

Knowing Obadiah Preview

Knowing Obadiah, Chapter 1: Bird's Eye Verses

> *And your eyes shall see, and you shall say, The Lord will be magnified from the border of Israel.* Malachi 1:5

Last week in my Wednesday night Awana class, I tasked my five fifth graders with collectively writing out as many books of the Bible as they could remember. They hopped to it, heads bent together as they worked.

"Genesis, Exodus, Leviticus," said Lisa, the scribe of the group.

"Don't forget Matthew!" Matthew contributed.

"Salms," "Efeseans," and "the Solomon guy" went down on the paper along with "all the Johns."

I beamed at their eagerness, Awana bucks at the ready to reward their efforts. When the flow ebbed to a trickle, I helped them along by pointing out that they hadn't remembered the book that starts with the letter O. They looked at each other, brows scrunched, then at me.

Joshua, ever the intrepid one, voiced the question written on every face at the table. "There's one with an O?"

A few months ago, before I began my study of the minor prophets, I probably would have made the same face. Little wonder, since *Obadiah* consists of a grand total of twenty-one verses. It's the shortest book in the Old Testament and the second shortest in the Bible. Even so, it packs a huge message, one I'm sad to have missed for so many years.

"Yep," I replied to the kids. "It's one of the minor prophets."

That clue didn't jiggle loose any memories, even though they gave it their best head-scratching effort. When I finally gave them the name, they all made sounds of "Oooh." The book's name was familiar, but (like many modern Christians) they couldn't bring it to mind or say what it was about. The poor book, Obadiah, just doesn't get the recognition its prophecy deserves—at least not from modern Christians.

At the time of its writing, however, I imagine the prophet's message made age splash. After all, what better news for the destroyed kingdom of Judah than to hear that the contributors to their downfall would be punished beyond oppression, beyond destruction? No, nothing as simple as devastation for the Edomites.

In payment for their actions against Judah, Edom would become "utterly despised" (Obad. 2), covered in shame, and "cut off forever" (10). Their own deeds would return on their heads (15), and, unlike Judah and Israel, to whom God always left a remnant, there would be no survivor left standing (18). Don't mess with God's Chosen People, y'all. Seriously, God is *not* cool with that.

Supporting Israel can be an important lesson to glean from this little book, but there's so much more to be had. One of my goals for this study is to further your grasp of how the major players in Israel's lineage and history knit together.

God really is the master weaver. So impressive. The book's backstory, including the bad blood between the Edomites and Israelites, goes back a thousand years, all the way to Isaac and Rebekah's twins, Jacob and Esau.

Because of that, the first half of this study will be dedicated to understanding the book's context in history and discovering God's marvelous hand in it all the way through. I trust you'll find the story and promises related in these twenty-one verses as fascinating and encouraging as I do and more familiar than expected.

Since I'm a girl who likes to know what's coming, outlines and bullet points are my jam. No surprises for me, please and thank you. So, over the next five chapters, here's what we'll be covering.

Part 1: Meet the players (v. 1)

- Key verses

- Who's Obadiah

- When's Obadiah

- Obadiah's audience

- Introducing Edom

Part 2: Book's origin story (10a)

- Jacob and Esau, the twins who started it all

- Thefts, blessings, and threats

- Esau's "blessing" fulfilled in Edom

Part 3: Edom's violence against Judah

- Judah's downfall (10a)

- Edom's hand in it (11–14)

- Ezekiel and Jeremiah weigh in

Part 4: Edom's violence repaid

- Arrogance and foolish boasting (2–4)

- Wrath prophesied (5–7)

- Wrath played out (8–9, 10b, 15–16)

Part 5: Judah's ultimate victory

- Three blessings (17–18)

- Three promises (17–18)

- Jesus Messiah will reign (19–21)

After glancing at the outline, you probably picked up on two repeated E words: Esau and Edom.

Esau, Jacob's hairy twin.

Edom, the nation that formed from his descendants.

Not your typical Bible study topics, huh? That's okay. Different is good. It means we're going deeper, digging past the comfortably familiar passages and books.

If you're looking for a tried-and-true Sunday school story, the Genesis account of Jacob and Esau is probably at the top of the list. From there, most of us take the right-hand fork in the road and follow Jacob's descendants into the formation of Israel and, later, Judah.

We forget all about Esau, his sons, and his sons' sons, called Edomites. We even forget to connect Edom with the twins of Father Abraham days. And have you ever tied the Edomites with those who threatened Jesus, Peter, and

Paul? I'm going to assume not. That ends here, my friend. We're taking the left fork, which leads down Esau's path.

In fact, over the next chapters, we'll get so far into the weeds of Esau/Edom and Jacob/Judah's thousand-year interactions, the sky might disappear for a bit. But have no fear, you *did* pick up a study on Obadiah, and when that sky reappears, our "eyes shall see, and [we] shall say, The Lord will be magnified from the border of Israel" (Mal. 1:5).

To some of us, Edom is an afterthought. Not so with Israel and certainly not for God. From Genesis to Malachi, from the first book of the Old Testament to the last, the Lord "loved" Israel and "hated" Edom (Mal. 1:2–3).

Here, the words *love* and *hate* don't mean affection and lack of. They mean "choosing for a special purpose[1]" and *not*. Yes, Israel is destined to play a particular role in world history, but God's eternal plan acted out on Earth extends further than the nation of Israel. The plan is to get a clear depiction of that through Edom and His treatment of their wickedness.

Better yet, through Edom, God emphasizes His loyalty to His children, to those who choose to follow Him and His ways.

That's me! And that's you, sister. Regardless of our earthly heritage, that's *anyone* who places their trust in Jesus as Savior, as the final verses of Obadiah (17–21) so gloriously state.

But I'm getting way ahead of myself. All in good time. For now, settle in for this fresh look at Esau, Edom, and their role in God's perfect plan.

What's up first? Read the book!

Because Obadiah is so short, I recommend you read it through several times. Personally, I listened to it being read aloud from my Bible app every morning while I dressed for the day, often hitting replay to listen to it again and again. I now have the book practically memorized. Bonus.

Confession. When I first read Obadiah, it didn't make much sense or seem to promise much in the way of take-away content. Maybe I'm a special kind of dense, but while I grasped phrases and concepts, I mostly didn't know which way to interpret some of the passages. Especially those last five.

Are the verses talking about Edom or Israel? (All the theys and thems made my head spin.) Is Obadiah referencing past events, present day (his), or is he prophesying about events yet to come (his or ours?)? Questions, questions, questions.

It wasn't until I'd consumed several commentaries that it began to make sense. Then, with a dozen lightbulbs going off over my head, I realized the book's length is no reflection of its complexity.

As I studied the book a verse at a time, my daily readings became clearer and clearer. There were a lot of *ooohh* and *ah ha* moments. By the time I'd finished my research, I had a fuller understanding of ancient biblical history and the relationships between neighboring nations. I had also uncovered another layer of God's awesomeness and had received a stark reminder that *God is sovereign.* In short, I came to love the book.

I pray the same for you. By the end of this study, you'll be an Edom and Obadiah pro, too. I promise. So hang tight, my friend. Trust the process and read on.

Key Verses

Our two key verses for Obadiah cover both God's judgment and His redemption. Declarations of judgment against Edom, as well as the reasons for it, make up the lion's share of the book.

Promises of redemption and restoration for Israel slide in at the end like punctuation. An exclamation mark, if you ask me. "And the kingdom will be the LORD'S," Obadiah finishes in verse 21. Makes a girl want to whoop a victory shout.

So few words. Such a powerful statement. And so simply delivered. "It's mine," says God through Obadiah. He doesn't need speeches to get His point across. He always gets the last word, and His Word is *fact.* The kingdom will be as He said. His.

God's indisputable rule over time, as well the events involving humankind, is a constantly repeated truth in Scripture. Hundreds of years before Obadiah picked up his quill, King David was singing about it in Psalm 9. This song can safely be considered prophetic, especially when cast in the light of the tragic events described in Obadiah, as well as God's vow of justice.

The Lord also will be a refuge for <u>the oppressed</u>, a refuge <u>in times of trouble</u>. And they that know thy name will put their trust in thee: for thou, Lord, hast <u>not forsaken</u> them that seek thee. Sing praises to the Lord, which dwelleth in Zion: declare among the people his doings. When <u>he maketh inquisition for blood</u>, he remembereth them: <u>he forgetteth not the cry of the humble.</u> (Ps. 9:9–12)

You can bet the captive Jews of Obadiah's day were singing this psalm to keep the faith. They would have clung to it as they read Obadiah's prophecy and looked forward to the day the injustices against them would be avenged by a supreme God.

This study's key verses touch on those exact topics.

Key Verse 1: Judgment against those who oppose God's children: "For thy violence against thy brother Jacob shame shall cover thee, and thou shalt be cut off for ever" (Obad. 10).

Key Verse 2: Deliverance for His children: "And saviours shall come up on mount Zion to judge the mount of Esau; and the kingdom shall be the Lord's" (Obad. 21).

Obadiah reminds us that life's disasters are not final. Restoration will come to those who seek the Lord, even if that's not until "kingdom come."

Great is thy faithfulness, Lord, unto us.

Pop Quiz:

Read Obadiah then write the number of a verse that:

1) intrigues you: _____

2) confuses you: _____

3) encourages you: _____

Find *Knowing Obadiah* at
AprilGardner.com/FireandFlame
or at any major online retailer.

Made in the USA
Monee, IL
19 October 2023